Selected by *The New York Times Book Review* and *School Library Journal* as one of the best children's books of this year.

GENTLEHANDS

The newest novel by M. E. KERR

"Kerr's earlier novels, splendid as they are, seem like a prelude to this story. It's a marvel of understatement, diamond insights, irony and compassion."

—*Publishers Weekly*

"There's no question that Kerr comes through with a real stunner that will leave you reeling with Buddy—and feeling for him through his first rude collision with the world beyond appearances."

—*Kirkus*

"Kerr at her provocative best."

—*School Library Journal*

GENTLEHANDS
by M. E. Kerr

BANTAM BOOKS
TORONTO • NEW YORK • LONDON • SYDNEY • AUCKLAND

RL 6, IL 6+

GENTLEHANDS
*A Bantam Book / published by arrangement with
Harper & Row Publisher's Inc.*

PRINTING HISTORY
Harper & Row edition published April 1978
2nd printing ...... June 1978
Bantam edition / April 1979
7 printings through October 1983

*Bantam Books are published by Bantam Books, Inc. Its trade-
mark, consisting of the words "Bantam Books" and the por-
trayal of a rooster, is Registered in U.S. Patent and Trademark
Office and in other countries. Marca Registrada. Bantam
Books, Inc., 666 Fifth Avenue, New York, New York 10103.*

PRINTED IN THE UNITED STATES OF AMERICA

H   15 14 13 12 11 10 9 8 7

To remember my friend,
Dr. Martha Wolfenstein,
1911–1976

1

I wonder what that summer would have been like if I'd never met Skye Pennington. They always seem to have names like that, don't they? Rich, beautiful girls are never named Elsie Pip or Mary Smith. They have these special names and they say them in their particular tones and accents, and my mother was right, I was in over my head or out of my depth, or however she put it. My father said, "She's not our class, Buddy." This conversation the first night I took her out.

I was in the bathroom, pretending to shave. I'm a towhead, like all male Boyles, and at sixteen my beard is not a burden; it's not even a fact.

My mother was just outside, in the hall, pretending to straighten out the linen closet.

Streaker, my five-year-old brother, was around the corner in our bedroom, pretending he could play Yahtzee alone.

My father was using the top of the toilet seat like a chair, while he discussed the matter with me.

"She's not in our class?" I said. "What does that even mean?"

I knew what it meant. It meant we lived year round in Seaville, New York, on a seedy half-acre lot up near the bay, and Skye summered on five oceanview acres at the other end of town.

Another thing it meant was that my dad was a sergeant in the Seaville police force, and Skye's dad was head of Penn Industries.

"Do you actually pay attention to that stuff?" I said, as if I never did.

"Buddy, that stuff is a fact of life." My mother's voice from the hall. "Sad but true."

"Inge, am I handling this, or are you?" said my father.

"Oh excuse me for living," my mother said.

"I thought you asked me to handle it."

"I asked you to talk to him."

"What is there to talk about?" I said.

"What there is to talk about is where the hell you're spending all your money!"

"Don't get mad at him, Billy," said my mother. "I said to talk to him, not to shout at him."

"It's my money, isn't it? I earned it," I said.

"Since when do you spend your money on clothes?" my father said.

"If you know where I'm spending my money, why do you want to talk about where I'm spending it?" I said.

"You're spending it on clothes like some girl!" my father shouted.

"He's spending it on clothes *because* of some girl!" my mother shouted.

"I don't spend one hundred and fifty dollars on clothes in six months' time," said my father. "You've spent that much in one month!"

"You wear a uniform half the time," I said.

"Buddy, *I* don't even spend that much on clothes in six months," said my mother.

I wiped my face with a towel and said between my teeth, slowly, "I do not plan to spend one hundred and fifty dollars every month on clothes. I just needed new things, that's all. I can't go everywhere in dumb, stupid jeans, old shirts, patched pants, and dumb, stupid worn-out shoes!"

"It's summer, for God's sake!" said my father. "Who are you expecting to meet?"

"He's already met her," said my mother.

"She must be some hotsy-totsy phony!" said my father.

"Well it's been nice talking to you, Dad," I said.

"I can't talk to you," he said.

2

"You've just proven that," I said.

He got up and sighed and stood for a minute with his hands on his hips. He looked miserable, but I didn't help him out any. He'd just had a haircut and he has these big ears, and he had that raw kid's look that was in all the old photographs of the days when he and my mother were first married. Whenever I looked at the family album I felt sorry for my father. He'd be standing in our yard, which didn't have any trees in those days or any grass; he'd be holding this little bundle in his arms with a little head sticking out of it (that was me) and he'd look like he'd sure bitten off more than he could chew. My mother was quite a beauty in those days and she looked sure of herself and up to settling down and being a wife and mother, but there was something about my poor dad that said he should have still been riding bicycles with the boys, or hanging around the pizza parlor making cracks at the girls who went by. He didn't look ready for the Mr. and Mrs. towels my grandmother Boyle had given them for a wedding present.

"I don't know, Buddy," my father said. He ran his palm through his short-cropped hair and shook his head. He never could talk very well about things and he hated it that he sometimes got mad when he was trying to.

"Don't worry," I said. "I'm watching it."

"Yeah," he said, as though he had his doubts.

"I didn't buy me a tuxedo yet," I said. I smiled at him.

He gave me back one of his red-faced, lopsided smiles and said, "That'll be next, a monkey suit. Huh?" He gave me a punch in my gut.

I feinted one near his jaw. "Don't worry," I said. "I won't make your mistake."

"What's my mistake?"

"Getting married before you were dry behind your ears."

"Oh I like that," said my mother. "Thanks a lot for that."

3

My dad laughed and sniffed and tried to land another one on me. I ducked and said, "Get outta here."

He threw his hands up in the air and muttered something like "oh what the heck," then walked out. So much for our talk.

When he went into the kitchen to get a bottle of beer, my mother followed him. I could hear them talking in low voices. I suppose she was giving it to him, but not really bad because she was always the first to say Dad had trouble expressing himself.

I went into the bedroom and started looking through all the new stuff I'd bought, while Streaker curled up in the top bunk and pretended to be asleep.

"I know you're awake," I said.

He didn't answer me.

"Maybe Mom should put you to bed every night around seven o'clock," I said. "You obviously get all worn out by this time."

He didn't rise to the bait.

I guess I bought so many clothes because I didn't know very much about clothes. Not *clothes*. I knew about putting on what everybody else puts on to go to school or hang around, but I didn't know what to show up in for my first date with Skye Pennington. I chose a pair of white slacks and a white shirt with this red belt. I had a white cotton jacket to go with it, so I decided to do a white number. My tan was started. I liked white with a tan.

Streaker was pretending to snore.

"Well, little bitsy teeny-tiny kids are always put to sleep by big people's talk," I said. Streaker still didn't bite. He stuck with his act. Once, while I was buttoning my shirt, I whirled around and caught him looking at me through his baby fingers, which he had over his face.

"Caught you!" I laughed, but he wanted more of a game. I wasn't up to it. I was too nervous about my date.

I was always giving myself lectures about being more of a big brother to Streaker. He was too little to tag along with me most places I went. Where we lived

4

there weren't any other kids his age nearby. He spent a lot of his time wandering around to neighbors' houses, like old Mrs. Schneider's up on Underwood Drive, where he always got fed fudge brownies. I'd vow to spend more time with him when I was home, but something always came up. After school was out, I got a job at The Sweet Mouth Soda Shoppe, and shortly after that Skye Pennington came waltzing in with her gang. From that day on my life seemed to have one focus, and I'd go over and over our conversations, sifting through them for meanings that probably weren't there, looks that probably didn't mean anything, whatever I could use to spin a fantasy with.

Then I just came out with it one afternoon. "I'd like to take you out Friday night."

"I'd like to have you take me out Friday night."

That was it.

My mother appeared in the doorway of the bedroom and said, "What are you smiling at?"

"I was remembering something."

"Where's Streaker?"

"He's in a coma up there," I said. "He did a swan dive off the bed and hit his head on the Yahtzee dice. I can't wake him up."

Streaker's little body was choking on suppressed laughter.

"Buddy," my mother said, "it isn't that you're not supposed to date girls who aren't in our class. It's just that if you need to go out and spend a whole year's savings on clothes to date one, she's not worth it."

"I won't know that until the night's over," I said.

"Oh yeah, what could make it worth it, huh? One hundred and fifty dollars. What could make it worth it?"

"Don't ask," I said.

"Buddy, don't get fresh with me." She put on one of her stern looks and folded her arms and stared at me. She always looked older than my dad, but when she put on weight the way she was doing at the beginning of that summer, she really added years to her

5

age. She was forty, but she looked five or six years older.

"I'm not getting fresh," I said.

"It sounded fresh." She has long blond hair which goes all the way to her waist, when it isn't done up on top of her head the way it was that night. She has the bluest eyes of any of us Boyles; we all have blue eyes, and she has the greatest smile. She and Streaker are the smilers in the family.

"I'm sorry if it sounded fresh. I wish everybody wouldn't worry so. I can take care of myself, Mom."

"I know that. Just don't turn into a snob like your grandfather."

I have only one living grandfather and it's her father, but she never calls him her anything; she doesn't even call him Dad or Papa. He lives in Montauk now, which is a twenty-minute drive from Seaville, but she never goes there to see him.

"*Jawohl!*" I said. "*Wie geht's?*" spitting out what little German I knew. My mother was actually born in Germany, but she left before she could walk or talk, and never knew her father. He didn't even look her up until she was a grown woman, never even tried to write her or write to anyone to find out if she and her mother were all right.

By the time he got around to caring about his daughter, it was too late. I think my mother hates him.

"One thing I can't stand is a snob!" my mother said.

"Grandpa Trenker doesn't seem like such a snob." I'd met him only twice, once when I was little, and don't remember; once when my mother took me to see him in Montauk. He lives in this huge house by the ocean. He seemed all right to me, one of these foreign types with the classical music going and a lot of talk about his gardens. I couldn't wait to leave, though, because my mother was so uncomfortable around him. She just thought I ought to meet him, she said; he is your grandfather, she said, and he doesn't have two heads or anything, so you'll see for yourself.

"Grandpa Trenker doesn't think his you-know-what smells," my mother said. She couldn't bring herself to

6

say the word "pee," so she made the expression sound worse than it was.

"Well I'm not going to turn into Grandpa Trenker, so don't worry," I said.

"Streaker," my mother said, "I know you're awake. Get down from there and put on your pajamas."

Streaker didn't move.

"All in white," my mother said, looking me over, smiling. "Streaker! Get down from there this minute and put on your pajamas!"

Streaker sat up and glared down at us. "I'm not going to sleep in those dumb, stupid old pajamas!" he blurted out.

"Little pitchers have big ears," my mother said.

"I'm not!" Streaker said. "I'm not going to wear those dumb, stupid pajamas."

"Good-bye, big shot," I said to him. "Good-bye, Mom. I have to rush."

"All in white," my mom said. "You look like Prince Charming."

2

"All in white!" Skye Pennington exclaimed when she greeted me. "You look like a waiter."

"The specialty tonight is rack of lamb," I said, swallowing my chagrin and borrowing some lines from my busboy days at Gurney's Inn. "The fish is fluke."

"You're the fluke," she laughed, touching my jacket sleeve with her long fingers, the nails pointed, and painted pink like the soft cardigan she wore over her shoulder. "Don't go away. I want Mom and Daddy to meet you."

She ran off with her long black hair bouncing down her back, and left me standing by the pool. In front of the pool house a trio was playing a squeaky rendition of the old Beatle song "Yesterday." It had never sounded worse. The other guests were milling around in little cliques holding drinks. I turned my back on them and pretended to be absorbed by the fantastic view of the dunes and the ocean, which were about four hundred feet away. I was sure I didn't know anyone there, anyway; most of them were older.

The name of the Pennington estate was Beauregard. We've got some summer neighbors on our street who call their place "God's Little Half Acre." They rent shares in it, and in June, July and August there are always a half dozen beat-up cars crowding the driveway. There were cars crowding the driveway at Beauregard, too. I'd never seen so many Mercedes in one place in my entire life.

To get to Beauregard, I'd had to thumb three rides, which took me only to the entranceway. Then I'd had to walk about a mile up to the house, if you can call a mansion a house. It came complete with an English butler named Peacock. He didn't come right out and say I looked like a waiter, but before I had a chance to say anything, he asked me if I was from Country Cook, which is a catering service. Then he started to direct me to another entrance.

I remember a story Oliver Kidd told me once about going to dinner in New York City with his uncle. They went to the Plaza Hotel, and Ollie was trying to pretend he always ate in places where there were maître d's hovering around and filet mignon for fifteen dollars on the menu. When the waiter asked them what they wanted for dessert, Ollie looked at the list and ordered Assorted Pies.

I had the idea I was probably going to do something like that before the night was over.

Skye seemed to be gone for a long, long time, and I was just beginning to think I couldn't maintain my pose of being this cool character enjoying the ocean view. I was shifting my weight from one foot to the other, shoving my hands in my pockets, taking them out again, licking my lips and combing my hair with my fingers when someone came up to me.

"One fish out of water meets another," he said.

I turned around and looked at him. He had on bright red pants, a red-green-and-white plaid jacket, and a bright green shirt. I'm six foot one and he came up to my shoulder. He was bald, and he wore these yellow-tinted glasses with a hearing aid attached. He was puffing on a fake cigarette, the kind smokers use when they first give up the habit. The cigarette glowed red when he breathed in on it. I figured he was about fifty, and I could smell a sickly sweet cologne or aftershave he had on.

"Oh yeah?" I said, because I couldn't come up with anything to say to the idea he saw himself somehow linked up with me.

"My name's Nick," he said.

I said, "I'm Buddy."

"You don't know anybody here, either, do you, Buddy?"

"I've got a date with Skye Pennington."

9

He made the cigarette glow. "A blind date?"

"No, not a blind date, either."

"You been dating her long?"

"Not that long." I was beginning to get a little steamed.

"I didn't think so."

"Why didn't you think so?"

He shrugged.

"Well why?" I persisted.

"Do you live out here?"

"Yes."

"Year round?"

"Yes."

"I thought so," he said.

"Why did you think so?"

"You're a townie," he said. "You live in town. That's what we used to call them when I went to college. We called girls we dated who weren't in sororities and lived in town, townies. You're a male townie."

"What's wrong with that?" I asked him.

"I'm not looking for anything wrong," he said. "I'm looking for explanations, that's all."

"I'm looking for *you*," a voice behind me said, and then Skye grabbed my hand. "Daddy," she said, "this is Buddy."

Yellow glasses moved away and I stared up at this gargantuan man with thick white hair, sea green eyes like Skye's, and a tan that made me look anemic. He got my hand in the vise of his fingers and pumped it hard twice, then dropped it. "I'm glad to know you, Buddy. Mrs. Pennington has an appointment and can't meet you. She sends her apologies."

"Pleased to meet you, sir," I said. I was wondering what kind of an appointment someone could have in the middle of a party, and glad that I remembered the sir. Ollie Kidd always said if you sir'd the girl's father, you were already ahead of the game.

"Daddy, we don't have to stick around here, do we?" Skye asked. Anything bad that had happened to me since I'd arrived at Beauregard was made up for by the way she looked: nearly as tall as I, thin with

10

a full figure most thin girls don't have, Skye was all in pink right down to her sandals; tan legs that were straight and strong looking—that long, shining black hair spilling down her back, her great, white smile. I wanted to grab her hand and run the length of the beach with her, so we'd never meet anyone else or get back for a long time.

"Where do you plan to go?" Mr. Pennington directed the question to me.

Skye answered it. "We're just going to drive around, Daddy, maybe go to some of the hangouts." It was the first mention I heard of driving around and I was about to say that I didn't have a car, when Skye said, "Can we take the Jensen?"

"What are the names of these hangouts?" Mr. Pennington asked.

I hadn't been planning to take her to them, but I answered, "The Surf Club, Dunn's, The Sweet Mouth Soda Shoppe." I'd planned to go to the beach, never figuring the beach was her backyard. The kids all hung around Main Beach, and I knew Ollie'd be there with his car. Maybe we'd get something to eat later at Dunn's.

"Do these hangouts serve liquor?" Mr. Pennington asked.

"Oh Daddy, every place serves liquor. What kind of a question is that?" said Skye. "We serve liquor, too."

"Do you drink, Buddy?" Mr. Pennington asked me.

"No, sir, I don't."

"Do you drive?"

"I have a license," I said, but I didn't say I was sixteen and couldn't drive after nine, and didn't have a car anyway. It was my first realization that I was younger than Skye.

Mr. Pennington said, "You can take the Jensen if Skye drives. You're to be back here at midnight, Skye."

"Will I turn into a pumpkin if I'm not?" She laughed.

"Do you understand, Buddy?" Mr. Pennington asked me.

"Yes, sir," I said.

Then he reached down and put his long arms around her and hugged her very hard, as though she was taking off on a cross-country tour.

"Be careful, baby," I heard him whisper. "I love you."

I didn't meet anyone else at Beauregard that night. Skye took my hand and led me through the crowd, chattering all the way.

"Mummy's appointment is with her spiritualist, could you die?"

"Really?"

"Yes, really. His name is Bachoo and he's into astral travel and everything and Mummy would leave an audience with the Pope if he showed up, which he just did. Daddy says he always shows up just when Daddy's flown in Dungeness crabmeat from the coast, which Daddy just did for this party, and there won't be any left, either, because Bachoo's The Human Hoover— that's Daddy's name for him—he just breathes in food like a vacuum cleaner sucking up dust."

Just at that point in her rambling, we passed the red pants and the plaid jacket in a cloud of that sickly sweet scent, with his yellow glasses turned toward me. "G'night, Buddy," he called after me.

"Good night," I said.

"Do you know Mr. De Lucca?" Skye asked me.

"I just met him."

"He's the token writer tonight," Skye said. "Mummy found everybody but a black. A writer, a couple of artists, this divine astrologist, and even a man who plays the bagpipes. We're lucky we don't have to be here for that. He plays 'Amazing Grace' off key, and it's just hairy to hear, I promise you!"

"That guy's a writer?" I said. "That guy in the yellow glasses?"

"His name's Nick De Lucca," Skye said.

"What's he written?"

"He's a journalist," Skye said. "Mummy found him through Bachoo. He did a story on spirituality in the Hamptons or some darn thing. Hey, the garage is this

12

way." She pulled me down a stone walk away from the house and then let go of my hand, as though now that we were alone it wasn't right to hold hands. Maybe she was just shy when she wasn't around a lot of people, I figured, because she stopped chattering, too. We walked along in the moonlight, silently, for a while. Behind us, I could hear the trio playing "Shine On, Harvest Moon."

"I've never been in a Jensen," I said, and immediately wished I hadn't said it. I'd never even heard of a Jensen, but I'd planned to play it cooler before I just blurted that out.

"That's all right," she said. "Most people haven't. It isn't your ordinary, everyday car." She fumbled in her bag for the keys while we walked toward a large, barnlike building. "Oh here're my keys," she said. "Are you happy, Buddy?" She stopped then and looked at me, taking me completely by surprise.

"Sure I'm happy," I said, sounding like some slowwit.

She looked at me for a moment, her eyes fixing right on mine, and I looked away, because it was too much. She was too much; the whole thing was, and I was beginning to think I wasn't enough.

She walked up very close to me and said very solemnly, "I want you to be happy with me, Buddy."

"Okay," I managed. I croaked it out actually. I didn't understand her, or I wasn't up to her, or ready for her, but I wanted to be. Oh how I wanted to be.

Then she did what I thought she was going to do and told myself of course she wasn't going to do that—she put her hands very gently on my face a second, looked into my eyes, and I felt her soft, moist mouth just for the sweetest, shortest time press against my mouth.

I didn't touch her, and before I had a chance to say anything she smiled, stepped away, touched something I didn't see, and the garage door opened, lights went on to display six sleek cars, one a Rolls. She moved toward the last one on the left, dark green. "The Jenny," she said. "Want a lift somewhere, sailor?"

I wondered if I'd ever be able to talk again, or walk

without my knees trembling, or breathe without my heart slamming into my ribs. But I got in beside her, and when she asked me while she was backing out where I wanted to go—"Make it someplace special, Buddy"—I heard myself answering in a very confident tone, "Montauk."

"What's there?" she said.

"My grandfather," I told her. Just like that, it came out of my mouth, and Skye let out a laugh that was like a whoop, and said, "Oh Buddy, that's subtle! I'm going to like you, Buddy Boyle, I can tell."

3

"Hello, Grandpa? This is Buddy." There was a long pause. Skye was parked at the corner waiting for me while I phoned him. I could see some guys walking back and forth admiring the Jensen, or admiring Skye, and Skye smiling at them. Why did she have to smile at them, I thought, and my stomach tightened; it would tighten all summer over any little thing like that, anyone coming near her.

"Buddy?" My grandfather finally spoke. "Ingeborg's boy?"

"Yes," I said. "I'm in Montauk."

"Is anything wrong?"

"Nothing's wrong," I said. "I'm just in Montauk."

"I see. I—" I couldn't blame him for not being able to think of anything to say. Our family had been about as interested in Grandpa Trenker since he'd moved to Montauk ten years ago, as we were interested in Rumanian gypsies or gamma rays.

"I suppose it's a lousy time to pay a visit," I said.

"Not at all," he said. "Is that what you want to do?"

"I have a girl with me," I said.

"How fortunate for you," he said. "Do you know the directions?"

He gave them to me, and warned me that at the end of his private driveway there'd be a chain across the road with a padlock attached to it.

"It isn't locked," he said. "Just undo it, then drive all the way to the end. I'll put on lights for you. You'll hear Mignon barking."

"Does he bite?" I said.

"She," he said. "No, she won't bite you. Are you coming right now?"

15

"Right now, if that's okay."

He said it was, and I ran from the phone booth to the Jensen. All the guys who'd been shuffling around the car stood there gaping at us as we took off, and I thought of how many times I'd been the gaper. Then I watched Skye's profile while she drove up Old Montauk Highway, and felt the chill as we neared the ocean, and smelled the salt spray. It was like a dream, I thought, and I wondered if it would always seem like a dream and never seem natural to be with her.

You couldn't see my grandfather's house from the road. There were woods all around, and after I undid the chain, we started up the long hill. His house sat right on the edge of a cliff overlooking the ocean. The first time I'd ever seen it—the only time—it hadn't been dark as it was that night, and all I could think of as I stared at it, formidable and superb standing there in the sun with the blue ocean stretched out beyond it, was that nobody related to me could live in that house.

"Nice" was what Skye said at our first glimpse of the place.

Grandpa Trenker had the yard bathed in light.

"Oh, and who's *he?*" Skye squealed as she got out and this shaggy dog came running to greet us.

"It's a she," I said. "Her name's Mignon."

"Hello, Mignon," Skye said, letting the dog jump up on her and lick her arm. "What kind of a dog are you? Are you an opera and not a dog, because I know an opera named *Mignon,* but I've never seen a dog like you!"

"She's both an opera and a dog"—my grandfather's voice—and he stepped out of the shadows then, walking toward Skye with his hand extended.

Skye took his hand. "I've never *seen* a dog like this!" she squealed again, and Mignon kept jumping on her. "What *kind* of a dog is this? I thought I knew every kind of dog there is! My mother, Mummy, used to raise green-eyed, all white Pomeranians, which are kind of rare—but what are you, honey?" Skye said to the dog. I was beginning to realize she chattered very fast when she was nervous.

16

"Down, Mignon!" my grandfather said sharply. The dog obeyed instantly.

"Mignon is a keeshond," said my grandfather. "And I'm Frank Trenker."

"I'm Skye Pennington. How do you do, Mr. Trenker."

"Hello, Grandpa," I said.

"Good evening, Buddy."

"A keeshond," Skye babbled on as we walked toward the house. "I've never heard of a keeshond and I've been dragged to dog shows since I was old enough to toddle, believe me. I thought I'd seen every breed there was, but a keeshond, oh Mignon, aren't you special, and I LOVE *Mignon,* the opera, too. '*Adieu, Mignon,*'" she sang, and my grandfather chuckled. They walked ahead of me.

My grandfather might be a snob, I thought, but he has something to be a snob about. Did you ever see the old, spooky movies on T.V. with Boris Karloff in them? He's this very tall, thin, very undaunted character, thick white hair, a mustache—my grandfather looks something like him, only he's not spooky. He's dignified, and confident, and you just know that in his day he was really something else, and he's still an extraordinarily handsome man. I'd turn around on the street to get another look at him, even if he wasn't my grandfather. He's that kind of man. You notice him; you know he's special in some way. He's in his sixties, but he's one of those men who you don't think of as an old man. When I went to Montauk to see him that time with my mother, I thought all those same things about him, but I was trying to see him through my mother's eyes, and I didn't let myself admire him. I tried to imagine how I'd feel if my dad just ducked out on me while I was growing up, and then reappeared and tried to say he was my father. I'd have had the same reaction, I guess: you can just take that father bit and stuff it!

But he hadn't done anything to *me,* had he? At some point bygones had to be bygones, and I guess we were at that point that night. I was, anyway.

My grandfather had this opera going on the stereo when we walked inside the house, and Skye gave another squeal and said it was her favorite aria of all, and she sang "*Un—bel—di,*" and did a little spin and clapped her hands. "*Madame Butterfly!*" she said.

She said to me, "Butterfly is singing 'One fine day,' Buddy. She's saying one day there'll be a thread of smoke rising from the ocean, and her husband's ship will come into the harbor, and he'll rush up to the little house on the hilltop to greet her."

"Very good," my grandfather said.

I didn't say anything, but I'd noticed that Skye realized I didn't know one opera from another, which didn't make me feel great even though it was true. About the only serious music we ever played in our house was Perry Como's version of "The Lord's Prayer."

My grandfather's house was filled with books and paintings and the kind of furniture my mother called "fancy antique stuff." Skye waltzed around admiring everything, and I remembered when I visited there with my mother, the thing that impressed me the most was the view of the ocean from the windows. Skye saw that view all the time at Beauregard. We couldn't see it very well in the dark, anyway, but we could hear the waves crashing down on the beach, and we could see the lights of the other houses arcing down the coastline.

There was a glass of wine on the table beside a large leather chair. In front of the chair, on the oriental rug, there was a bag of sunflower seeds. My grandfather explained he was just about to fill his bird feeders.

"The birds like to feed early in the morning," he said, "before I'm up. I'm a night owl, so I fill the feeders before I go to bed."

"Oh, you'd love Mummy, my mother," Skye said, "she's a bird lover, too, and she keeps track of every bird she's ever seen, about one hundred and fifty varieties, and when I was a kid she'd drag me out here to the walking dunes at Oysters Pond to spot birds. I mean, what did *I* care about birds, but now I wish I'd

18

paid attention because I don't know an oriole from a robin."

"It's never too late to learn," said my grandfather.

"I'd really like to learn," Skye said. "I really admire birds, they're so *free*. I mean, they *symbolize* freedom."

"Far from it," said my grandfather.

Skye said, *"What?"*

"I said far from it. Birds look free but they're not, you know. They're very restricted. They're prisoners, really, of their own territory. They can't move easily from one territory to another."

Skye looked at him a moment, eye to eye, carefully, the way she'd looked at me in the driveway at Beauregard when she told me she wanted me to be happy with her. Then she said, "I really admire you, Mr. Trenker. You're subtle. I mean, you're really subtle —and I like all of this—" her arms sweeping out to indicate the whole room, everything. "I do."

When Skye called something or someone subtle, it was her highest compliment, I gathered. I just sat on the couch and let them talk, congratulating myself for bringing her there. I remembered an English teacher we had once describing something called "borrowed glory" to us. Borrowed glory was when you couldn't think of a way to say something, so you got out Bartlett's *Familiar Quotations,* looked up "love" or "fear" or "patriotism"—whatever subject you had on your mind—and you copied down what Shakespeare or Emerson or someone famous had said about it, and put that into your composition as a quote. This teacher used to say just because you could find a quote about something didn't mean you'd really expressed *yourself.* It just meant you'd borrowed glory. He said there were all sorts of ways to borrow glory. If your family was rich and you were conceited about it—that was borrowing glory, too, because you hadn't done anything to make them rich—you were just coasting on their abilities.

So that night I was borrowing glory by letting my grandfather make the impression on Skye Pennington,

19

instead of trying to impress her with my own personality.

Well, thank God for borrowed glory, I thought. Thank God I had someone in my family to borrow it from, because all the while I sat there watching Skye, I told myself I wasn't going to let her slip through my fingers. Whatever it took to keep her in my life, I was going to do it . . . even if it meant learning about opera, which had always sounded to me like a lot of people screeching around in German or Italian with music drowning them out until they could get their breaths again.

We spent a lot of that evening—or they did—talking about animals. My grandfather was this great animal lover. He had a whole pot of plain spaghetti cooked which he put out on his back patio for raccoons to have. He had a light fixed so we could see them sneaking in from the woods, one by one, taking the spaghetti in their little hands and winding it all around themselves while they sucked it into their mouths. They looked like little masked bandits, and a few of them stretched out on their backs like clowns and fed the spaghetti into their mouths in long strings. They took marshmallows from his hand, and he let Skye feed a few to them, and she looked over her shoulder at me with this expression of sheer joy on her face, as though she'd never done anything so fantastic in all her life.

About eleven o'clock I said we'd better leave, remembering Mr. Pennington's order that Skye was to be home by midnight. Skye got up and went into the bathroom, leaving me with my grandfather, the first time in my life I'd ever been alone with him. I couldn't think of anything to say, and we just sat there for a moment while he took a sip of his wine and looked across at me.

"Do you think you impressed her, Buddy?" he finally said.

"Well, *you* did." I mumbled, and his remark had made my face red.

He didn't say anything, so I said, "It was borrowed glory, I guess."

"I'm happy to lend it to you," he said.

"Thanks."

"How is your mother?"

"She's fine," I said. "We're all fine."

I was hoping he wasn't going to try and make some excuse about what he did to my mother, what he didn't do for her, or try to explain it, and I needn't have worried. He didn't mention her again. He sat there sipping his wine while I drank what was left of my ginger ale and wondered how anyone could stand opera —there was another one playing, some woman shrieking, then a man bellowing some sort of answer.

"You know, Buddy," my grandfather finally said, "you can get there on your own, once you're pointed in the right direction."

"Get where?" I said, but I knew what he was talking about. He knew I knew, too, and didn't even bother explaining where.

"I'd be happy to point you, if that's what you want," he said.

"What do you think of her?" I said.

"She's very beautiful," he answered. *"Very."*

"But beauty's only skin deep, huh?" I said. "That's something my mother is always saying."

"On the contrary," he said. " 'Spend all you have for loveliness,/Buy it, and never count the cost;/For one white singing hour of peace/Count many a year of strife well lost./And for a breath of ecstasy/Give all you have been or could be.' "

Somebody spouting off poetry always made me a little self-conscious, unless it was a teacher who had to for a class assignment or something. I couldn't think of anything to say.

"One of your American poets wrote that," said my grandfather. "Sara Teasdale."

"What you're telling me is she's worth it, even if I do have to bring her out here to impress her."

"What I'm telling you," he said, "is that *you're* worth

it, too; that with a little polish, you won't have to bring her out here, although she's always welcome."

"I haven't even been out of Seaville," I said, "except to go to Disneyland once with my folks . . . and Block Island another time with my dad."

My grandfather smiled. "It isn't where you've been," he said. "An ass who goes traveling doesn't come back a horse."

"She's also older than I am," I said. "I don't know how much older, but she is."

"A woman you love is always older than you are, even when she's younger."

"I don't know what that means," I said.

"When you love a woman, she seems secret and mysterious," said my grandfather, "things you associate with the full bloom instead of the bud."

"She's rich, too," I said. "The Penningtons have tons of money."

"Obstacles are challenges for winners, and excuses for losers," said my grandfather.

"I never thought of it that way," I said.

Skye came back from the bathroom then, and my grandfather walked us down to her car.

"I hope I see you again, Mr. Trenker," said Skye. "This has been such a super evening, and Mummy's not going to believe a raccoon ate out of my hand. I don't even believe it myself. I can't wait to spring keeshond on her, too. She'll die if she's never heard of one, you know, it's like telling the Pope he doesn't know all his cardinals or something."

"Come again," my grandfather said, looking straight at me, "if you want to."

"If we *want* to!" Skye exclaimed. "Does a starling want one of your sunflower seeds!"

"Not very much," said my grandfather. "He has trouble getting the shells open."

"The one time I wanted to show off and say a starling or a blue jay or something besides just a plain bird, I pick the wrong bird." Skye laughed. "I like you so much, Mr. Trenker. You're subtle!"

"I try to be," my grandfather said.

22

All the way back to Beauregard, Skye did seventy, talking nonstop about him.

"You don't mind going fast, do you, Buddy?" she asked me.

"It doesn't feel like we're going too fast," I told her, but it did, and we were, and I knew I wasn't going to do anything to stop it.

4

I tried to convince Skye to let me drive to Beauregard with her that night, and hitch a ride back to my house, but she wouldn't hear of it. She dropped me and took off like a rocket. I saw my father standing in our driveway by his Toyota, smoking a cigarette, watching me. He was in uniform because he was working nights that week.

"That was a Jensen she was driving," I said. "Did you ever hear of a Jensen?"

"Did she ever hear of a speed limit?" he said.

"Oh, *Dad*."

"It isn't funny, Buddy," he said.

I stood there and he stood there and then he said, "Where'd you go?"

I didn't want to tell him then. He wasn't in the greatest mood and I didn't want to open that whole can of worms at the end of a beautiful evening.

"We just rode around," I said.

"Rode around at eighty miles an hour?"

"She wasn't doing eighty."

"She was doing close to it," he said. He took a drag on his cigarette and twirled his car keys in his hand. "Buddy, if your social calendar isn't too full, I'd appreciate it if you'd do something with Streaker tomorrow."

"I work until two," I said.

"And after two?"

"I was going clamming with Ollie."

"Take Streaker with you," he said. "Okay?"

"Okay," I agreed.

"Streaker hangs around his mother too much," my father said.

24

"I know that. Okay."

He gave me one of his friendly punches and opened his car door. "I've never even heard of a Jensen," he said.

"Neither had I," I said.

"Well, anyway, did you have a good time?"

"Yeah."

"Your mother's asleep on the couch," he said. "Don't wake her up, she's beat. We started to panel the playroom tonight."

The playroom was actually the garage. My father had built a wooden floor there, and they were fixing it up for Streaker and me.

"See you tomorrow," I said.

My mother was in her robe with the afghan over her. I guess after she'd finished helping him with the paneling, she'd begun work on his scrapbook, because it was open on the coffee table, with newspaper clippings and a pot of glue next to it. Every time my father's name appeared in *The Seaville Citizen,* my mother would clip the article, underline his name, and paste it on a page. His name was in the paper almost every week. Stuff like "Sergeant William Boyle arrested G.L. Jones of Fireplace Drive at 11 A.M. Wednesday morning for speeding and driving while intoxicated." The whole scrapbook was filled with things like that.

I tiptoed past her, went into the bedroom, and undressed in the dark. Streaker was snoring, and I got under the covers and began reliving the whole evening in as much detail as I could make myself remember. I was glad I didn't have to face my mother, and go into the visit to Grandpa Trenker. The next morning I beat it out of the house before anyone was up, and rode my bike to The Sweet Mouth Soda Shoppe, ready for work.

In the summer we always had a fairly good early-breakfast crowd on nice days. Everyone was eager to get to the beach. It was a warm, sunny Saturday, so even the owner, Kick Richards, was hustling around in the kitchen, flipping pancakes and throwing bread into

25

the toaster. Kick used to be an actor until he married a local widow about ten years older than he is. He's in his early forties, a former drunk who claims pot changed his life. He usually comes in when it's crowded, and when the crowd thins, rolls himself a joint and smokes out back. Any of the employees who want a favor from Kick wait until he's had his joint; then he's open to all requests and suggestions.

The one thing Kick hates is to have employees use the phone in his office, which is this dinky room about the size of a small bathroom. There is no pay phone, so if you want to make a call, you either have to walk around the corner to the front of the A&P, or get Kick to relent.

Around ten thirty that morning we had a slow period, and I saw Kick head for the back steps. I waited about ten minutes, then went out to confront him. Kick's a nice-looking man, on the short side and very thin, with longish blond hair and round brown eyes. Ollie's mother calls him "This failed actor who married poor Ginny Townsend for the little money she has left"—he doesn't go over too big with the locals.

He was sitting on the steps listening to the news over WWRJ on a pocket transistor.

"Jesus, that was funny," he said to me.

"What was?"

"The announcer just said the police are using a time-tested strategy on the man in Wilmington holding those people hostage—waiting. Waiting is a strategy?" He laughed. "That's some strategy. Waiting. All those years I wasn't working in New York, I was really using a time-tested strategy, Buddy. I was waiting."

"Yeah," I said. When Kick smoked grass he always picked apart what he heard and found something funny about it.

"Kick," I said, "if you were falling in love with somebody and couldn't even make a fast phone call to them, how do you think you'd feel?"

He sat there thinking it over.

"You know what you're going to be someday, Buddy?" he said.

26

"What?"

"A *gozlin*," he said. "Do you know what a *gozlin* is?"

"A goose?"

"That's a gosling," he said. "You're going to be a *gozlin*, rhymes with Roslyn. It's Yiddish."

"What's it mean?"

"An unmoral, unethical person," he said. "A swindler. When you're finished calling her make sure my office door's closed."

Peacock answered the phone and said Miss Skye was swimming in the ocean.

"Would you care to leave a message?"

"Just tell her Buddy Boyle called," I said, because I couldn't see telling Peacock to ask her if I could see her that night. All the way back from Montauk I'd wanted to ask her what she was doing the next night, but I'd been afraid she'd say she was busy, and that would spoil the time we'd just spent together.

I began to get into a small panic, wondering how I'd get ahold of her before evening. Somehow I had to get hold of her before I went clamming.

When I went back on the floor, Ollie was sipping a Coke at a table by the window.

"I want *all* the details," he said. Ollie and I have been hanging around together since fourth grade. He's this redheaded guy with freckles where most people just have pores, buck teeth he dreams of having capped someday, and a build like an Olympic weight lifter. He's a tackle on the Seaville High football team, and last year some poor runner from Westhampton High collided with Ollie and was unconscious for ten minutes.

"All *what* details?" I said, trying to ignore the fact the woman behind him was waving her hand at me, trying to order breakfast.

"Did you make out?" Ollie gave me his chipmunk grin, and I sighed and shook my head.

I said, "I'll be glad when you date more than three times a year, so you don't have to live through me."

"No kidding, Buddy, how'd you do?"

"WAIT-*TER!*" The woman behind Ollie was working herself into something.

"I can't go into it," I said. "Streaker's coming with us today, okay?"

Ollie nodded and I felt Kick come up behind me and grab me by my belt. "Get your ass over to that customer!" he said. "And tell your baboon friend this isn't the local watering hole."

"Now I know how come you call this place Sweet Mouth," Ollie said, and he was mad, his face was all red. He tossed a quarter on the table and shoved his chair back hard.

"Oh dearie," Kick feigned this apologetic tone, "don't tell me we're losing *you* for a customer!"

I felt sorry for Ollie because I knew he was supersensitive about the way he looked and the baboon crack got to him. It always got to me when someone picked on the way Ollie looked, because I'm considered really good-looking, and I didn't do anything to get this way. Ollie went storming out of the place, and I gave Kick a dirty look that he shot back to me in spades.

"This isn't the local pool hall, Buddy! Tell your friend to find another hangout!"

"Oh go roll another joint," I said under my breath, and Kick said, "I don't know what kind of a wisecrack you just made, mister, but the next time I do *you* a favor hell will freeze over!"

It was going to be one of your beautiful days, I told myself, at the rate things were going; it was going to be one of your all-time glorious days.

Then a groupie crowd descended on the place (they're these summer people who rent one house and sell about nineteen shares in it)—at least a dozen, with more straggling in a few minutes after that—and I was struggling with trays of eggs and pancakes and French toast until I thought my shoe leather would burn holes in Kick's floor. Groupies tip about ten cents on a three-dollar order, too, so I seemed to be running behind in every way.

Suddenly, just as the noon whistle blew, and every

town dog milling around in front of the A&P down the street started howling, I looked up and saw her.

"Do the dogs always howl along with the whistle?" she said.

"Hi!" I said.

"Hi!"

She was all in blue, right down to her sandals. I guess she specialized in wearing all one color, and she had this great perfume on, and that smile, and she just stood there and I just stood there, and the jukebox was roaring out some rock number, and the whole place was babbling around us, waiters calling out: "Two over easy, o.j. and one black."

"I came to get you," she said.

"I'm working," I said.

"I'm shopping," she said. "What time are you through working?"

"Two," I said.

"I'm going to take you for a swim," she said. "Would a swim make you happy, Buddy?"

"I guess it would," I said.

"Don't guess with me, Buddy," she said.

"BUDDY!" I could hear Kick behind me.

"Someone's calling you," she said. "I'll be parked outside at two sharp. Okay?"

"Okay," I said.

Before I'd left the house that morning, I'd stuck a note up in Streaker's bunk telling him to be ready at two thirty.

So much for promises, and clamming.

"What in the HELL is wrong with you?" Kick asked me.

"Nothing!" I lied.

5

The pool house at Beauregard is bigger than the house I live in. Skye directed me to one of the four dressing rooms; it was about the size of the bedroom I share with Streaker. There was a table and couch and chairs, a rug on the floor and paintings on the walls. On the table there was a slim silver vase with a white rose in it, and about two dozen photographs in gold and silver frames. Skye was in most of the pictures, along with her older brother, Ogden Pennington, Jr., who was traveling in Europe that summer. There were pictures taken through the years of the family—on skis, on surfboards, in horse-drawn carriages, near Christmas trees, and rolling eggs down long green lawns. There were pictures of them on ships and getting off planes, in golf carts and on horseback. On our table at home there's just one photograph, of Streaker and me, the dollar-nineteen Woolco color kiddies' special, in a plastic frame.

On the way to Beauregard, Skye had said not to worry about the fact I didn't have a pair of swim trunks with me, she'd fix it. She'd made a phone call from the Jensen, on a real phone, not a CB radio, and sure enough there was a pair of navy trunks and a large navy towel laid out for me on the couch. We'd mostly listened to a tape of Barbra Streisand on the way there. I hadn't felt much like talking; I was still feeling guilty that I'd lied to my mother, and told her I had to disappoint Streaker because Kick needed me to work the afternoon shift.

I looked really crummy in my old clothes. About the only thing I had on that wasn't a rag was a new red sweater I'd bought the week before. I was glad to ditch my clothes and get into the trunks, sorry I hadn't worked a bit on more of a tan because everyone around the pool was the color of bronze.

Just outside the dressing rooms there was this large room with tables and chairs, a bar and an enormous gold mirror covering a whole wall. My bare feet sank into the thick rug, and I saw Skye stretched out on a chaise, waiting for me, in a two-piece white bathing suit with a light blue monogrammed *P* on the bottom half. The light blue *P* was on everything around the pool: pillows, tablecloths, ashtrays, matchbooks and sun pads.

"Mummy's dying to meet you!" Skye said, and three tiny dogs yapped around near her feet as we walked out into the sun. Skye said they were Papillons, which meant butterfly in French. They weighed in at about four pounds.

There were about twenty people lounging around. In the center of the pool, on a float, I saw the man with the yellow-tinted glasses lying on his back, the false cigarette glowing as he sucked on it. Skye led me up to a chaise with a light blue-and-white parasol attached to it, and a chubby, deeply tanned, silver-haired woman under it. She was wrapped in a large white towel with the light blue *P* embroidered on it. She was sipping orange juice and reading a book called *The Stars' Stars*.

She greeted the butterfly dogs first. "Janice! January! Little Ophelia. You girls settle down or mean old Peacock will have to take you in, and you'd miss everything. You wouldn't like that one bit, would you?"

"Buddy," Skye said. "This is my mother."

"How do you do, Mrs. Pennington."

"Buddy *who?*" She put on bright blue tinted sunglasses and looked up at me.

"Buddy Boyle," Skye said.

"What sign are you, Buddy Boyle?"

"I'm a Gemini."

"Mercurial, amusing, communicative," she said. "Mr. De Lucca out there is a Gemini, too, with Leo rising. That's why he's a journalist."

We all automatically looked toward the float, and

31

then Mrs. Pennington said, "He can't hear us talking about him without his hearing aid. I've often lamented that I cannot close *my* ears as easily as I can my eyes."

Skye sat down and so did I, and Skye said to me, "Mr. De Lucca is out here in Seaville on some mysterious mission. He won't tell anyone about it, will he, Mummy?"

"I hope he doesn't," said Mrs. Pennington. "I like mysteries, and secrets and puzzles and games. Would you like to play backgammon with me, Buddy?"

"I don't know how to play," I said.

"You can tell a great deal about someone by how he plays backgammon," said Mrs. Pennington. "Skye here gets careless after a while and fails to protect herself. That's the way she is in life, too, I'm afraid. Aren't you, darling?"

"Oh I take care of myself, Mummy," Skye said.

"What *do* you play, Buddy? Do you play croquet?"

"No," I said. "I play Yahtzee with my kid brother sometimes. I play Monopoly."

"I don't like Monopoly at all," Mrs. Pennington said, "unless I get both Boardwalk and Park Place right away."

"The green properties are pretty good," I said.

"North Carolina Avenue and those?" she said.

"I've won a lot of games with those," I said.

"Rrrrrreally?" she said.

There was a splash as Nick De Lucca rolled off the float and kicked his way toward the ladder.

"I hope Mr. De Lucca isn't bored here," she said. "They say the way to entertain artists and writers is to feed them or amuse them or shock them. Well we fed him; we've done what we could."

"I'm going to introduce Buddy to everyone," Skye said while Mr. De Lucca walked toward us, rubbing his head with a towel.

Mrs. Pennington said, "Hand him his shirt, dear, on the back of that chair. His hearing aid is in the pocket."

De Lucca took the shirt, hooked up his hearing aid after he put the shirt on, then dried his glasses on a corner of the shirt. "Why do people have heated pools?" he said. "Hello, Skye." Then to me, with a lilt of surprise, "Well, hello there."

"Do you two know each other?" Mrs. Pennington said.

"We met the other night," De Lucca said.

"Buddy's been telling me the most interesting things about Monopoly," Mrs. Pennington said.

"I didn't think anyone could tell a Pennington about monopoly," De Lucca said, and Mrs. Pennington clapped her hands and giggled.

"Oh we aren't discussing oil, Mr. De Lucca," she said. "I leave that to Ogden. We were discussing the game of Monopoly." She picked up some knitting from the table beside her, placed it on her lap and began working the needles.

"Sit down, Mr. De Lucca."

He said, "What are you making?"

She held her knitting up for us to see. "Can anyone guess?"

"Sweaters," I said, "for Janice, January and Ophelia."

"I'm knitting only one thing, Buddy." I was sure I'd guessed right. It was blue and white of course.

"*A* sweater for one of the dogs," I corrected myself.

"I suppose it looks like a sweater," she said, "but it isn't. Mr. De Lucca? You love mysteries."

"I pass," De Lucca said in a bored tone.

"Why they're golf-club covers!" Mrs. Pennington said.

De Lucca winced and drew in on his fake cigarette.

Skye took me around and introduced me to people. They sat in little cliques of three and four, by the pool, and we finally joined some kids our age, three girls and a boy. His name was Connie as in Conrad. Anyone in my crowd called Connie would have done something about it—fast—use his middle name or go by a nickname, but Connie Spreckles didn't seem to mind his name at all. Skye told me later he was a San Francisco Spreckles, whatever that meant. I just said "Oh" as though it made perfect sense.

33

Everyone took great care to say my name at the beginning or end of anything they said to me, like "Do you really live out here all year, Buddy?" or "Buddy, is there anyplace to go besides The Surf Club?" I could tell they were all bending over backwards to include me, even though there'd be long passages of time when they'd talk about people I didn't know, and places I'd never been to. They all referred to The Hadefield Club a lot, as though it was their second home. I'd never even been inside it. It was this real snob place down the road from Beauregard, right on the ocean, the kind of place that didn't let many Jews in, or anyone without tons of money. Around town we called it The Hate-Filled Club.

I don't remember whose idea it was to play "Whose Is It?" but apparently they'd all played it before and thought it was a hilarious game. One of the girls went to the pool house and brought back an assortment of clothes found in the dressing rooms. Then another girl would hold up something: a shoe, a belt, a shirt, a cap —and everyone would try to guess from the smell, the label, the look of the object, who had worn it.

I saw my new red sweater in the pile, and didn't think anything about it until the girl named Rachel picked it up and said, "The label says Made in Korea." Then she rolled her eyes to the heavens and said, "Now, *really,* how tacky can you get? And it's Orlon!"

"It's the yard boy's," Connie said.

"It smells like a yard boy's," Rachel said, holding the armpit to her nose and making a face. I'd worn the sweater half the morning at Sweet Mouth.

"It's mine," Skye said.

"Oh sure it is," one of the girls said. "Orlon's never touched *your* sacrosanct skin, my darling!"

Skye stood up and snatched the sweater out of the girl's hands and said, "This is a jackass way to spend our time! Who wants to race to the beach?"

Connie understood then and said something that sounded like "There's nothing wrong with Orlon," but he was on his feet and running after Skye, and the other girls followed. Rachel stayed behind with me.

"I don't feel like a race to the beach," she said.

She put the sweater on a chair and sighed. We didn't say anything for a while, although I was trying frantically to think of something to say. She finally said, "I hate myself, you know."

"I think I'll take a swim," I said.

I got up and dove into the pool.

Later, when I was dressing to go home, Skye knocked on the door and slipped inside.

"Mummy loves you," she said, beginning to chatter fast the way she did when she was nervous. "Now we're going to have to get out the Monopoly set and let her try the green strategy or she'll never let us rest, honestly, Mummy can be *relentless,* and poor Daddy *hates* games, he can't play backgammon or croquet. I mean, he plays golf but that's about *it!*"

"I suppose you've got something on tonight?" I said.

"Oh and do I wish I didn't, Buddy, because it's the most boring thing in the world, a dance at The Hadefield and I can't get out of it because Daddy has a table reserved and it's this e-*nor*-mous sit-down dinner, but I'll see you Sunday night, won't I?"

"If you want to," I said.

"I want to," she said. She looked at me that way she had of looking at someone so intensely and I couldn't hold it, and dropped my eyes before she did.

She said, "I want to remember the color of your eyes, Buddy."

I just wasn't used to that stuff at all, and I pretended to have to tie my shoelaces which were already tied, and she probably thought I didn't feel anything because she went back to chattering—something about not having time to run me home and how she hated sit-down dinners and wearing long dresses, it took her hours to put her face on, and would I mind if Mr. De Lucca gave me a ride?

"I'll see you Sunday," I said when De Lucca called into the pool house, "I'm leaving, Buddy!"

"Promise me?" she said.

"What do you mean?" I said. "Of course I promise

35

you." For some reason I had the feeling I was this close to crying or something stupid, I didn't even know, but I walked out of the dressing room without saying anything else, or looking back, just went, depressed as hell.

De Lucca was driving this little white Fiat convertible, and I climbed in beside him, while he made the phony cigarette go red, puffing on it, not saying much as we headed down the long driveway, and then down Ocean Road to town.

I could smell the sickly sweet scent he wore and I breathed in the air on my side of the window, wondering if it was possible that I was going to puke from the stink.

"What's your name, anyway?"

"Buddy," I said.

"Buddy what?"

"Boyle," I said.

He took the fake cigarete out of his mouth and looked at me for longer than someone driving a car should gawk across at his passenger.

"Is your father a cop?"

"Yeah."

"William Boyle?"

"Yeah. I'm Junior."

"No kidding," he said.

"No kidding."

"Well," he said.

"Well, *what?*"

He didn't answer me and I didn't give a damn because I was too down to care what was on De Lucca's mind.

When I finally got home, I saw my father sitting on our front porch, where he almost never sat, in a way he almost never sat, with his legs crossed and his arms folded, and I didn't even have to see the expression on his face to know he was waiting for me, and it wasn't going to be pretty.

6

"Where've you been, Buddy?" my father said.

"Kick asked me to work overtime."

"That's where you were until now?" My father looked at his watch. It was six o'clock.

"About four I took a swim," I said.

"I see."

"It was too late for clamming by then."

"I suppose it was," my father said.

Then my mother called out to us, "Come and get it!"

"I better wash up fast," I said.

"On the double," my father agreed.

I collided with Streaker as he was leaving the john. "Hey, Streaker," I said, running my hand through his hair. "How's it going?"

"I just combed my hair—*don't!*"

"You combed your hair, but you didn't flush," I said.

"*You* flush," he said.

"Streaker, you get back in here and flush!" I said.

"Oh let him alone," my mother called in.

"He never flushes!" I said. But I was really angry because I knew Streaker was hurt that I didn't take him clamming, and it made me feel guilty. I knew he hadn't flushed purposely. What I thought about while I washed up was: What if I'd really *had* to work overtime? What if it hadn't been a lie? What if I'd come home beat from a double shift of work and my brat brother decided he'd just get into a snit and not flush, not say anything about how hard I'd worked, nothing! It wasn't *my* idea to have a brother; it was their idea. They were trying for a girl and they got another boy, and because it was a boy, I was supposed to take over and help raise him! What was fair about that?

We always ate in the kitchen. About the only time we didn't eat in the kitchen was Thanksgiving dinner and Christmas dinner, when we ate in the dining room. The rest of the time there was this empty room with a lace tablecloth on the table and four chairs set around it, and a silver bowl in the middle filled with wax fruit. That made a lot of sense, too, and for some reason that night it teed me off. I guess I was just in a foul mood, anticipating everyone else's. But when I walked into the kitchen and sat down at my place, things seemed normal. My mother was humming and serving up spaghetti with clam sauce. My father was breaking the toe off a big loaf of Italian bread. Streaker was sounding off about the fact he liked "sketti" and meatballs better than "sketti" and clams.

"Where'd you go for your swim?" my father said after we all began eating.

"I went out to Skye's."

"You didn't have your suit with you," my mother said. "You didn't go swimming without your suit, I hope."

"They had a suit for me," I said.

"Who's 'they'?" my father said.

"Her family," I said. "They call the place Beauregard."

"This is delicious sauce," my father said.

"It doesn't have too much garlic?" my mother asked.

"It's perfect," he said.

"I like sketti with meatballs better," Streaker said. "But I hate sparrow grass."

"Well we're not having asparagus," said my mother.

"We're having it sometime," Streaker said, "because I saw it."

"We're having it tomorrow," said my mother.

"I'm not having it because I hate it!" Streaker said.

"I'll eat yours then, I love it," I said.

"You're stupid!" Streaker said.

"Don't call me stupid, Streaker," I said. "I don't like it."

"Don't call me stupid, I don't like it," Streaker said. "You're stupid."

"Eat your dinner, Streaker," my father said.

"What do you mean they'd had a suit for you?" my mother said.

"They have just about anything you want at Beauregard," I said. "Their pool house is bigger than this place."

"Well la-di-da," said my mother.

"They have a marble staircase," I said, "and this butler named Peacock."

"La-de-da-de-da," said my mother.

"They have a heated pool and a six-car garage."

"Ver-*ry* fancy," said my mother.

"There's a Rolls in the garage," I said.

"What's a Rolls?" my mother asked.

"A Rolls-Royce," my father said. "It's a car."

"Oh a Rolls-Royce. Why didn't you say so? Even *I* know what that is," my mother said.

"They have these little dogs called Papillons, which means butterfly in French."

"Pass the salt," my father said.

"One's named Ophelia. One's named Janice. One's named January."

"January's a month, stupid!" Streaker said. "January comes before February."

"Mrs. Pennington was knitting something by the pool and I thought they were sweaters for the dogs, but she was knitting golf-club covers," I said. "That's a new one on me, golf-club covers."

"They looked like sweaters?" my mother said.

"They looked like little dogs' sweaters, but they were golf-club covers."

"There's not too much garlic in this," my father said. "It's great!"

"I'm glad you like it," my mother said.

"It's delicious!" my father said.

"Everything has monograms at Beauregard," I said. "There's a *P* on everything. Everything's blue and white."

"I like a *lot* of color!" my mother said.

"The *P* is for Pennington, of course," I said.

"What does Mr. Pennington do?" my mother asked.

"He has oil wells, I guess."

"Oh oil wells," my mother said. "How nice for him."

"They go to Europe and all that stuff. Ogden Pennington, Junior, that's Skye's brother—he's traveling in Europe this summer."

"Pass the butter," my father said.

"They play backgammon and croquet. They play Monopoly, too, but Mrs. Pennington says she doesn't like to play unless she gets Boardwalk and Park Place right at the beginning."

"Streaker, tuck your napkin under your chin, you're going to spill sauce down the front of you," my mother said.

"I told Mrs. Pennington I liked to get North Carolina and the greens, and she couldn't believe it. She said she's going to try it."

"Well good for her," my mother said.

"She's into astrology and stuff and she said Gemini was—what'd she say again?" I tried to remember. "She said we communicate, something like that."

"You're certainly communicating tonight," said my mother.

"She said we communicate and we're amusing, or something."

"Well good for you," my mother said.

"You know how you've got just one picture out on the living-room table?" I said.

"Yeah?" my mother said.

"They have hundreds of them on this table in the pool house. They're all in silver and gold frames. I guess they don't just shove them in albums the way we do. They just frame them and put them out."

"In the *pool house?*" my mother said.

"It's not like a pool house, really; it's bigger than this place."

"So you said," my father said.

"It really is, and they've got these thick carpets and

paintings. You'd never think it was just someplace you changed into your bathing suit."

"Do you want more spaghetti, Bill?" my mother asked.

"I've had enough, thanks," said my father.

"Buddy?"

"I've had enough, too," I said.

"Thanks," my father said.

"Thanks, Mom," I said.

"I've had enough, thanks, Mom," Streaker said. "Can I watch T.V.?"

"Finish what's left on your plate and you can," my mother said.

"I hate clams!" Streaker said. "I hate what's left on my plate!"

"You hate everything!" I said. "You're turning into a pain in the ass, Streaker!"

"You shut up, stupid!" Streaker said.

"Don't ever say 'ass' in my presence again," said my mother.

"I'm sorry," I said. "How come he gets away with calling me stupid every other word out of his mouth?"

"Because you *are!"* Streaker said.

"Don't call Buddy stupid," my mother said.

My father pushed his chair back. "Buddy, I want to explain something to you about the yard when you're through."

"I'm through now," I said.

"Buddy, you hardly ate," my mother said.

"May we be excused?" my father said.

"Can I watch T.V.?" Streaker said.

"Okay, okay," my mother said. "Don't mind me, I'm going to finish my dinner."

My father and I went out the side door and walked back toward the toolshed.

"We've got a mole digging up the lawn, see the holes?" my father said.

"Why did we ever plant this kind of grass?" I said. "It comes up like hay." I was thinking of the soft, long green lawn at Beauregard.

41

"This grass is okay," my father said.

"If you like hay for grass," I said. "You ought to see the grass at Beauregard."

"Buddy," my father said, "turn around a second."

"What is it?" I turned around and faced him.

What it was was a punch to my neck, so hard I fell down from the weight of it. I just sat there looking up at his eyes, which were blazing. His face was the color of a ripe tomato. His hands were balled into white knuckles.

"Get up!" he said.

I got up and he socked me again. I reeled back, but caught my balance and stayed on my feet. My heart was slamming against my ribs and I stared at him while he just stood there watching my face with this look of revulsion in his eyes.

"You're very full of yourself, aren't you, Buddy?"

"What's got into you?" I said. I began backing away, but he kept coming toward me, slowly.

"I'll hit you back!" I warned him.

"If you do, I'll mop up the place with you!" he said. He was actually hissing the words at me like an angry snake: "You—just—stand—*still*."

I did.

He let his hands drop to his sides, but the fingers were still knotted into hard balls. "Golf-club covers and pool houses!" he snarled. "Thick carpets and everything monogrammed with *P!*"

"It's not my fault they're rich," I said. "And what's wrong with being rich?"

"A Rolls in the garage!" he said.

"So what?" I said.

"Little dogs that mean butterfly in French!" he said.

"Okay, I'm a little impressed," I said. "I've never met people like that. I'm a little impressed."

"You're too impressed!" he said.

"I know that," I said. "Okay."

"You're so impressed you lied, Buddy. I went by Sweet Mouth at two fifteen. Your bike was there but you weren't!"

"Okay," I said. "I lied."

"Why?" my father demanded.

"She came by to get me at two," I said.

"And you jumped, just like one of her trained dogs!"

I didn't say anything.

"The hell with Streaker, your bike, your mother, me—you had to hightail it over to Beaublahblah!"

"I'm sorry, Dad," I said.

"So am I!" he said.

Then he said, "You're to spend every single night right here for the next two weeks! Is that clear, Buddy?"

"It's clear," I said.

"I brought your bike home on the back of my car," he said. It was a ten-speed Peugeot that he'd given me for my birthday. My old bike was a three-speed Sabre, and my father'd agreed to buy me the Peugeot if I'd promise to take good care of it. One hundred and eighty dollars is a hell of a lot of money for a bike, he'd said.

But I wasn't paying much attention to that. I wasn't even paying attention to the fact that that was the first time he'd ever belted me and really meant it. I was too busy remembering that I'd promised Skye I'd see her Sunday night.

7

Our family isn't very religious, but my mother goes to
Mass nearly every Sunday morning.

My father had worked all night; he was asleep in
their bedroom. Streaker was still in his pajamas, eating a bowl of cereal in the living room, watching
"Josie and The Pussycats in Outer Space." I'd played
Yahtzee with him after the blowup in the yard with
my father, until it was his bedtime, letting him win
five games out of nine.

Sunday was the only day I didn't work, so I was
hanging around in my shorts, waiting for it to be eleven
o'clock, the time I figured it'd be okay to call Skye.

"Can we go to the bay?" Streaker asked me. He
had a milk mustache and a wet cornflake on his pajama
top.

"We might," I said. It was one of those beautiful
summer mornings in June. Down at the bay there were
already kids swimming out to the raft, and sailboats
dotting the horizon.

I looked at my watch. It was ten forty-eight.

"What do you mean we might?" Streaker said.

"I'm not making any promises I can't keep this
time," I said.

"We don't have to wait until Mom comes home,"
he said. "She said I could go if you took me."

"I know that," I said. "I have to make a phone call
first."

"Then can we go?"

"Maybe," I said.

"When are you going to make your phone call?"

"In a few minutes."

"Why don't you make your phone call now?"

"Streaker," I said, "do you mind letting me do things my way?"

"If you shout you're going to wake up Dad, and then Dad will be teed off and we won't be able to go to the bay."

"Don't talk with a mouth full," I said. "Do you think I want to look at all that garbage you haven't swallowed yet?"

I looked at my watch again and decided I'd try Skye even though it wasn't quite eleven yet.

I went into the kitchen and used the wall phone.

"Miss Skye will call you back," Peacock told me. "She's finishing her breakfast."

I gave him the number and paced around the kitchen waiting. I wanted to answer the phone on the first ring, so it wouldn't disturb my father. I'd heard him complaining to my mother early that morning that he'd had a hell of a night with DWI's all over Montauk Highway. That meant people driving while intoxicated. Saturday nights in summer there was a lot of that, and a lot of accidents because of it. I could never understand anyone getting behind the wheel of a car drunk. I'd probably do a lot of dumb things in my day, I always told myself, but that wouldn't be one of them.

Streaker came out to the kitchen and got out the stool and stood on it while he rinsed out his cereal bowl. Then he pulled out the dishwasher and stuck the bowl inside.

"Shall I put on my bathing suit?" he asked me.

"Sure," I said. "If we don't go to the bay, you can run under the sprinkler in the yard."

"I'm not going to run under the dumb sprinkler," he said.

"Do what you want to do," I said, and the phone rang.

"*Bonjour, cheri,*" Skye said.

"*Bonjour,*" I said.

"*Come va?*" she said.

"No speakety Spanish," I said.

"That was Italian!" She laughed.

"Spaghetti," I said, "ravioli, pizza."

45

"Fettucini," she said. "Did you think about me last night?"

"Un petit peu," I said.

Streaker was standing under me, scratching his belly and looking up at me with his face wrinkled up.

"Just a little bit?" Skye said. "Oh I'm going to commit defenestration on myself."

"Whatever that is," I said.

"That means I'm going to throw myself out the window," she said. "It's one of my Uncle Louie's words. We played words-of-twelve-letters-or-over last night at dinner, and Uncle Louie knows millions of them and he said I was an infracaninophile, which I bet you don't even know the meaning of."

"I don't."

"I didn't either. It means underdog lover. Uncle Louie says all Americans are infracaninophiles, and I'm a living example. Well I'd hate to be a dead example, I said, if I'm going to be any kind of an example of anything, I'm glad I'm a living example."

"About tonight," I said.

"Come over right now and we'll talk about tonight," she said.

"Right now?"

"We're going to have *dimanche déjeuner* on the beach at one, and we could swim before and I could give you your present. Would you like that, Buddy?"

"What present?" I said.

"Come and find out," she said. "Hurry!"

There was a click.

I hung up, too.

Then I picked Streaker up and whispered in his ear, "Hey, I've got a secret."

"Tell me at the bay," he said.

"Part of the secret is we're not going to the bay," I said, and then I put my hand over his mouth and said, "Shhhhh. Now listen. This secret is about tonight."

"What is it?" he said.

I picked the cornflake off his pajama top. "Tonight we're going to have a magic mystery hunt right here

46

in this house. We're going to hunt for a secret box containing tiny little secret things."

Streaker was pouting. "What tiny little secret things? I'd rather go to the bay."

"Not when you see the tiny little secret things," I said. I didn't know what the tiny little secret things would be, but I'd come up with something!

He squirmed in my arms and I put him down. "Streaker," I said, "try to understand something."

"What?" He was rubbing his eyes with his tiny fists the way he did just before he started bawling.

"Streaker, I'm in trouble," I said.

"What trouble?" He put his fists down and looked at me wide-eyed.

"I can't explain it now," I said, "but you have to help me."

"How?"

"You have to let me go now and not make a fuss. I have to get myself out of trouble. I'm counting on you, Streaker."

"Will Daddy have to arrest you if you don't get out of trouble?"

"It isn't that kind of trouble," I said. "It's worse."

"Worse than against the law?" he said.

"Don't ask any more questions," I said. "Just help me out, will you?"

"I guess so," Streaker said.

"Just keep what I've said a secret between us, okay?"

"Okay," he said.

"Don't tell Mom and don't tell Dad."

"Okay."

"I have to go and straighten it out, and when I come home we'll have a magic mystery hunt. Okay?"

"Okay," he said.

He followed me back to our bedroom while I changed into a pair of white pants and a striped T-shirt. I made sure the shirt wasn't Orlon but plain 100% cotton, and then I slipped into a pair of sneaks. I didn't need a sweater.

While I dressed, I said to Streaker, "When I was

your age I didn't have a brother, and I had to do everything by myself. How'd you like that?"

"I wouldn't like it," Streaker said. "Where do you have to go now?"

I put my finger to my lips. "Shhhhh, Streaker, we can't talk about it anymore. Just let me get out of here and take care of it."

"What'll I tell Mom?" he said.

"Just tell her I'll be back for supper."

"You're not going to have dinner here?"

"I can't," I said. "Just tell her I had to go out and it was okay with you. Got that?"

"You were going to eat my sparrow grass so I didn't have to," he said.

"Streaker, you're not helping me. Don't you think I'd eat sparrow grass if I could? I love sparrow grass!"

"Okay, Buddy," he said.

"That's my boy," I said, and I kissed him, and he wiped my kiss away, grinning with embarrassment.

"I'll turn the sprinkler on for you," I said.

Then I stuck two dimes in his piggy bank because I felt like a real rat.

8

Once I got to Beauregard, I always seemed able to put my own life out of my head, and just wallow in theirs, with Skye. Beauregard was like a drug; so was she. If a fleeting image of Streaker playing under the sprinkler by himself crossed my mind, it was soon erased by the sight of a flotilla of waiters carrying blue-and-white beach umbrellas down to the dunes, along with wicker picnic baskets with blue-and-white ribbons attached to the handles. The guests were beginning to arrive for the *dimanche déjeuner,* which just meant Sunday lunch in French.

Skye was all in yellow this time, yellow short shorts, a yellow shirt with the tails knotted around her tan midriff, and yellow sandals. We sat for a while by the pool talking. Connie Spreckles was there and so was Rachel, but Skye gave me all her attention.

"When do you want your present, Buddy?"

"I don't want a present," I said. "You didn't have to buy me a present."

"That's why I bought you one, because I didn't have to."

The Papillons were playing around by our feet, and Peacock was passing by with a huge silver bucket filled with bottles of wine.

"After you left yesterday afternoon, I called Mark, Fore and Strike in East Hampton, and told them exactly what I wanted for you, and made them promise to deliver it to me right away, which they did, because God knows I practically support them single-handed in the summer."

"Okay," I said. "What is it?"

She reached under her chair and pulled out a gift-wrapped package, placing it on my knees.

"Thanks," I said. "What is it?"

"Open it."

"Okay."

"I hope it's your size. You can return it if it isn't."

I tore off the ribbon and lifted the lid from the box.

"It'll be perfect for tonight, Buddy."

"Tonight?" I took it out of the tissue paper.

"We're having a hot-dog-and-marshmallow roast tonight."

It was a navy blue sweater, cashmere.

I held it up the way Rachel had held up my Orlon sweater the day before.

"Whose is it?" I said. I smelled it. "It smells very expensive. It must be Peacock's."

Skye laughed.

"Thanks," I said.

"Do you like it?"

"Sure I like it."

"Do you love it?"

"I'll probably sleep with it," I said.

"Oh you love it that much? I hope you won't sleep with it on the first date because that's gross."

"No. I'll wait."

I was embarrassed because I knew then how embarrassed Skye had been for me when we'd played the game in front of her friends.

"You're a little embarrassed," Skye said.

"You've got the wrong boy," I said. "All donations are gratefully accepted."

"Don't be," she said. "After all, I didn't have to work my tail off at Sweet Mouth to pay for it."

That remark just made it worse, but I got past it and laughed and loved her green eyes watching mine and told myself however long it lasted, I might as well enjoy it, because I doubted anyone like her would ever come my way again.

Skye wasn't the first girl I'd ever gone around the bend over. I'd had crushes on girls since I was thirteen. But she was worlds away and a far cry from

LuAnn Derby or Karen Suchanik, both of whose idea of flirting was to put Wind Song behind their ears and sit there.

We went into the pool house and changed into our suits (I'd brought mine with me this time), and she knocked on the wall separating our dressing rooms and called out, "I can say everything I want to say to you now because my door's locked and you can't come in and get me."

"What do you want to say?" I called back.

"Everything!"

We raced down to the dunes and I splashed into the ocean after her. We played in the surf, jumping the big waves, letting them carry us into shore, then rushing out to greet the new ones. All along the beach, people were watching the Beauregard waiters set up the umbrellas and backrests for the picnic, standing at a discreet distance while the Penningtons' guests settled down to enjoy the *dimanche déjeuner*.

If that was lunch, I was King Kong. Everyone had his own picnic basket; inside was a half chicken, cheese, potato, salad, deviled eggs, ham rolled up with watercress and mashed avocado inside, spareribs, an apple, grapes, and a thick wedge of chocolate cake. There were cold Cokes for the young people and cold white wine for everyone else. At our house they'd be just finishing Sunday dinner: steak with mashed and asparagus. Chocolate ice cream for dessert.

Connie and Rachel listened to tapes and sunbathed after lunch, and I slept for a while in the sand, on my stomach, until I felt Skye sitting on my back. "Do you want me to teach you backgammon?" she said.

We played enough games for me to begin to get the hang of it. There were a lot of backgammon games in progress while the waiters collected the picnic baskets. Peacock appeared to take the Papillons out of the sun and back to the house. People walking along the beach stared up at us in wonder, crossing back and forth several times, some of them.

"Will you whisper provocative things in my ear at the hot-dog roast?" Skye asked me.

51

I'd been putting the hot-dog roast out of my mind.

"I don't know if I can come."

"You don't have to come, you're here."

"I don't know if I can stay."

"I'll have to get handcuffs," she said.

"I don't know," I said.

I excused myself to go back to the pool house john, and saw a phone on the bar.

I dialed, heard my father bark "Hello!" and hung up, even though I knew he always barked hello, it didn't mean anything, particularly. He began the four-to-twelve shift that week. I looked at my watch. It was three fifteen. Another fifteen minutes and he'd be gone. I hung around the pool house, waiting, sitting on the barstool flipping the pages of *Time* magazine.

At three thirty-five my mother answered.

"Did you just call here a while ago, Buddy?"

"Of course I didn't just call there. Wouldn't you know if I'd just called there?"

"Somebody called and hung up and your father said he bet it was you."

"It wasn't me."

"Where are you?" she said. "Don't tell me. I know."

"Mom," I said, "they've asked me to stay to dinner. They're having a hot-dog roast."

"Your father said you're to be right here at night, for two weeks."

"Mom, he wouldn't have to know."

"What?"

"He's not going to be there, is he?"

"What are you suggesting, Buddy, that I lie for you?"

"I'd lie for you."

"Don't ask me to lie for you."

"I would for you."

"You promised Streaker some kind of magic mystery thing, too."

"Mom, Streaker is your kid. He's not mine. I didn't have him, you did."

"I didn't promise him anything magic or mysterious, Buddy, *you* did."

"Put him on the phone."

"Buddy, I can't lie to your father."

"Mom, I'm with nice people at a nice place."

"What does that mean?"

"Just remember that and don't worry about me. Tell Streaker he can have my baseball mitt. Tell him it's his."

"What does *that* mean?"

"Just tell him," I said.

Then I put the telephone's arm back in its cradle.

I don't know when things started going wrong that night. The nearest I can trace it back is when Mr. De Lucca walked up to our bonfire and sat down. We'd all been back and forth to the beach all day. Some people had left, some had stayed, some had played Ping-Pong up at the pool house or napped, played croquet or swam in the pool, and some new faces had joined the night party. There were little bonfires going all along the beach which the waiters had built, and we all sat around in little groups eating, listening to tapes, wise-cracking. I was just getting the hang of carrying on a conversation with Connie and Rachel and the others. It was all a matter of one-liners. Someone would say something about reality, and someone else would say "Reality is a crutch." Or someone would make a re-mark about anarchy, and someone else would say "Isn't anarchy against the law?" I used one of Ollie's old sayings when Connie told Rachel he thought she was really evil. I said, "Evil is just live spelled backwards." They all laughed, and Rachel tried to swat me with her espadrille.

We were going along like that when De Lucca sat down with us, tuning in his hearing aid, his glasses a ghastly yellow by the firelight, his phony cigarette glowing.

Skye was telling a story about how outraged her Uncle Louie was that there were Jews allowed in The Hadefield Club now. At the sit-down dinner there the night before, there was a table behind the Penningtons filled with the guests of a Mr. Abraham Plotz.

53

"I know Samantha Plotz," Rachel said. "She goes to Wood Hollow with me."

"Oh but wait!" Skye said. "She has a sister. Can you guess what the sister's name is?"

"Samantha Plotz." Rachel giggled. "I love her *dearly*, but what a name!"

"The sister's name is worse," said Skye. "The sister's name is Regina."

"Regina Plotz," Connie said, and he hugged his knees and rocked as he laughed.

"Samantha and Regina Plotz!" Rachel said. "The Plotz sisters!"

Everybody howled, and De Lucca watched us, sucking his fake cigarette, the glow going off and on and off and on.

"Uncle Louie says Ruth Plotz maybe, Adele Plotz maybe, Sara Plotz maybe—but *Samantha* and *Regina?*"

"I know a girl called Victoria Finkelstein," Connie said, as though there was nothing at all funny about a boy called Connie Spreckles.

"I'll tell you a story," said Skye. "Did you ever hear the story about the Jewish Santa Claus?"

"What about the Jewish Santa Claus?" De Lucca spoke up.

"Well," Skye said, "this Jewish Santa Claus comes down the chimney, see, and he says, he says—" Skye's shoulders began to shake and she had to get control to continue. "He says 'Want to buy any toys, kiddies?' "

Everyone cracked up but Mr. De Lucca, who never smiled anyway, unless it was a slight, slanted, sarcastic smile.

We sat around for a while singing to some old sixties song on the tape, and Rachel said she'd written a song. Connie got her to sing it. It was about falling in love with a falling-down fellow ("I'd just be feeling mellow, we'd be doing the town, then he'd fall right down, my falling-down fellow"). She said it was actually a poem she'd written while she was dating this boy who drank Thunderbird wine all day from a Coke can. She said he was a teenage alcoholic.

"I love to write poems, and make them songs," she said.

De Lucca spoke up suddenly. "I know a poem that should be a song. It was written by a teenager, too, a girl about your age. It's called *Gentlehands*."

He recited the poem while we all sat by the firelight and listened.

> *I can see your beauty*
> *But you can't see mine,*
> *And you have a gun.*
> *The only music I hear*
> *Is what you play for me.*
> *It is beautiful, too,*
> *But it does not speak*
> *To you about me.*
> *You listen and smile.*
> *I wait to die,*
> *And call you Gentlehands."*

"Wow!" Rachel exclaimed.

"That's subtle!" Skye said.

"What's it about?" Connie asked.

"Why does he have a gun?" I said.

"He has a gun because he's guarding her," De Lucca said.

"But he's playing music for her," Connie said.

"He's playing music to taunt her."

"Is she in prison?" Skye asked.

"It's like a prison," said De Lucca.

"What did she do wrong?"

"She didn't do anything wrong. She was only fifteen years old."

"Then what's she in prison for?" I asked.

"She's in Auschwitz," De Lucca said.

"Why does she call him Gentlehands?" Rachel asked.

"Everyone called him that. It was an irony."

"In *Auschwitz* did you say?" Connie said.

"Yes. Auschwitz."

"The concentration camp?"

"Yes," De Lucca said. "Her name was Roselina De Lucca."

"Was she Italian?" I asked.

"She was my cousin," De Lucca said. "She lived in Rome until they took her away."

"Who took her away?" Connie asked.

"The Germans, of course."

"Why?" Skye said. "She wasn't Jewish."

"She *was* Jewish," De Lucca said. "I'm Jewish."

Skye put one hand over her eyes and grabbed my hand with the other.

"What happened to her?" Rachel asked.

De Lucca stood up then. He said, "She was murdered." He gave us a small salute and sauntered away.

"Get me out of here," Skye said to me. "I just want to get out of here, Buddy."

"I've actually got goose bumps," Rachel said, and Skye and I were already on our feet and starting to run.

9

It was Skye's idea to drive to Montauk this time. I phoned my grandfather from Beauregard and he said he'd be delighted to see us again. Skye drove like a bat out of hell, talking a mile a minute all the way.

"I'm not prejudiced," she kept insisting, "and no one in my family is but Uncle Louie. Daddy calls Uncle Louie 'The rich man's Archie Bunker.' Did you ever watch 'All In The Family,' the T.V. series with that bigot, Archie, and his ditzie wife, Edith? Sure, we laughed at it—it's a comedy—but Daddy knows a lot of Jewish people, they come to our house and everything."

"De Lucca was just sitting there waiting for you to hang yourself," I said, watching the speedometer, praying to God my father wasn't anywhere near the Montauk Highway that night.

"How was *I* supposed to know he's Jewish? I doubt Mummy knows it. We just thought he was Italian."

"He's an Italian Jew," I said.

"I never even think of Italians being Jewish, do you? I thought all the Jews in those concentration camps were Germans. I mean, I've always felt terrible about those concentration camps, Buddy. I even did a theme once on that Anne Frank who kept the diary, and got an A plus on it!"

"Just forget it," I said.

"I'm trying to, Buddy. I honestly *never* tell jokes like the Jewish Santa Claus one. It just popped into my head and I could die!"

"If you keep talking about it, you won't be able to forget it."

"Don't mention this to your grandfather, Buddy, promise?"

"I won't."

"I think it's Uncle Louie's influence," she said as we turned onto Old Montauk Highway, and speeded along with the moon shining down on the ocean in the distance. "Uncle Louie really hates anyone ethnic, I mean, he *does:* blacks, Jews, even the Irish."

"Great," I said.

"He's the family joke he's so prejudiced. Daddy says it's because he's short and the only way he can look down on people is by looking down on their race or religion. Do you know Daddy even gave money to Israel?"

"Just forget it," I said. "We're here."

One of the first things my grandfather commented on was my new sweater, which really pleased Skye. He was wearing a black turtleneck sweater and tan corduroy pants, with boots that looked like he'd just polished them. There was a bottle of wine on the table next to his chair and a nearly empty glass. He was carrying this very fancy long pipe with what looked like flying horsemen sculpted on it.

"Daddy collects pipes," Skye said. "Daddy's got a Charatan, Mr. Trenker, do you know what a Charatan is?"

"Yes, I do."

Skye said to me, "A Charatan is the most expensive pipe in the world. It costs twenty-five hundred dollars!"

My grandfather smiled. "Well not exactly."

"It really did cost that much, Mr. Trenker."

"A Charatan is a straight-grain briar," said my grandfather, "and it would sell for around the figure you mentioned, but it's not the most expensive pipe in the world. This pipe, for example, is worth a great deal more, not that I'm practicing one-upmanship. . . . This is a hand-carved block meerschaum, imported from Turkey."

"What did *it* cost?" I said.

"It would be worth about eight thousand dollars," said my grandfather, and Skye hit her forehead with her hand and let out a long whistle. I just sank my hands into the pockets of my pants and strolled around basking in the idea I had a grandfather who could top the Penningtons on something.

He put an opera on for Skye called *La Traviata,* and then he asked us if we'd like a Coke.

"Love one!" Skye said.

My grandfather started to go and get two, and I said, "I wouldn't mind having a glass of wine." Sometimes when my mother and father are celebrating something like a promotion for my father, or their wedding anniversary, they have Cold Duck for dinner, and I have a glass.

"I didn't know you drank wine," said my grandfather.

"We have it with meals," I said.

"I'll bring a glass for you," said my grandfather.

"I love it here," Skye told me when he went into the kitchen. She began singing along with this character on the tape, *"Un di felice,"* and I watched her, happy that she was getting into a more relaxed mood. I loved it there, too. It was sort of my answer to Beauregard. I didn't even mind the music, and I remembered all the times my mother and I would make fun of the opera we'd sometimes get by mistake on the radio Saturday afternoons. My mother would pretend she was an opera singer and sing in this falsetto, throwing her head back and beating her bosom with her fist, and I'd pretend to keel over and die from a poison dart or whatever it was men died of in those things. If my father was home he'd call in, "Turn off the screech owls!" and we'd yell back, "Don't you want any culture?"

My grandfather appeared again carrying a Coke for Skye, and an empty glass for me.

"Pour yourself a glass," he said.

I put my hand around the bottle and began pouring, and he said, "Wait a minute, Buddy."

"What?"

"Always grab a bottle of wine by the neck," he said,

"and never fill the glass to the top." I couldn't remember how my father grabbed the Cold Duck, but he always poured the wine to the top of the glass.

My grandfather watched me while I did it the way he'd suggested. Some wine dribbled down to the tabletop, and he said next time I should turn the bottle just so, to catch the drippings before they spilled on anything.

Then I tasted the wine and it wasn't at all like Cold Duck; it was pretty bitter, but I pretended it was the best wine I'd ever had, which it probably was.

I suppose when you live alone you become a creature of habit, because after we'd sat around for a while talking, my grandfather jumped up and said it was time to fill the bird feeders. He said the raccoons didn't come until very late on Sunday nights because a neighbor down the way was out on weekends and left his garbage out. "But I have to attend to the feeders," said my grandfather, "because I do every night at this time."

I was beginning to feel high, not on the wine, particularly, but because it was such a great place, and he was the way he was, and Skye kept smiling at me, trying to hold my eyes with hers for long looks. When my grandfather carried the sunflower seeds out to the feeders, I went over and sat beside Skye, and I guess it was the wine then that made it easy for me to start kissing her. We just kissed and held each other while the opera played, and the sound of the waves crashing on the beach below came through the open windows.

"I'm crazy about you," I whispered into her soft, long black hair.

"Oh Buddy."

"I am."

"I am, too."

We were both whispering, and excited, and I sat back and tried to get control of myself, because I didn't want to be embarrassed when my grandfather returned. I looked at her face and she wasn't smiling and neither was I. I couldn't stop myself and reached for her again, and I don't know how long our lips

60

pressed together while we held each other very hard, but I heard my grandfather clear his throat and we both sprang away from each other.

"Don't be uncomfortable," he said, because I guess we both looked that way. He went and sat down in his chair and smiled at us.

"I never really knew anything about that sort of thing when I was your age," he said.

"Didn't you have a girlfriend?" Skye asked.

"I was too busy being educated. I was raised a Catholic, very strictly, and it was my father's wish for me to be a priest. It was a very long time before I ever loved a woman."

"How old were you when you finally did?" Skye asked.

"Much too old," he chuckled.

"Were you out of your teens?"

"I was divorced, and no longer a young man." He had one of his pipes in his hand and he was filling it the way someone does before launching on a story. Skye sensed that and urged him on.

Then he told us that he'd traveled a lot and very long distances until he met the only woman he'd ever loved, in Cuba. He said she was very beautiful, with long black hair like Skye's, only she was a woman, not a girl, and she had a mystic quality about her, a "fatalism" my grandfather called it. She loved all animals, as my grandfather did, particularly birds.

"Carla was her name," he said. "She believed that birds were in tune with nature, that they had more psychic dimensions than man. Man, she would tell me, is too busy computing data from his five senses to pay any attention to his supersenses. The reason man, most men, seem to think telepathy and such psychic phenomena are strange, is because there is just too much to cope with. Their brains receive so many impressions they can't grasp the deeper knowledge of life as animals can."

"Fascinating!" said Skye. "Mummy would love you, Mr. Trenker!"

"The birds that came to Carla's yard were unlike

61

any I have ever seen before or since, rare and extraordinary ones of many colors and songs. We watched them for hours. We were just happy watching them together, as though it was our own special pageant."

"Did you marry her?" Skye asked.

He shook his head. "I wanted to, though. I wanted nothing more."

"What happened?" Skye asked.

While he got his pipe going, I poured myself another glass of wine.

"One day at dusk we saw these two very large white birds gliding over the water. We'd never seen anything like them. Were they swans, some form of giant seabird? I don't know. We watched them, entranced, and Carla said they seemed like omens; they had a dazzling brilliance and their great white wings were spread but seemed unmoving, and they soared and dipped and glided in the wind, *beautiful!*"

"And then?" Skye said.

"And then the next day I came up the hill, after being in the city for many hours, and I smelled something very familiar that I didn't want to believe was the odor, the stench of something burnt-out. But it was. Her house had burned, and she hadn't been able to escape."

"Oh no," Skye said.

"I stayed there for a long while. A month? Two? Maybe more, living in a part of the house that had survived, continuing to feed our birds. I never saw the large white ones again."

I was thankful Skye was with me when my grandfather told that story, because I was never good at listening to anything like that. I was never able to think of anything to say. I just kept drinking the wine and letting them talk, half hearing what they were saying after a while. My grandfather was telling her about some famous psychiatrist named Carl Jung who believed there was an intelligence beyond individual intellect, what our American Indians called "deep-knowing." My grandfather said he believed it was how animals and birds perceived life, and he talked again of the great white birds, and the woman's death, and the relation of the two things.

I remember Skye trying to wake me up and get me on my feet. I remember my protesting that I couldn't go home; I'd had too much of the wine. I couldn't face my father drunk, on top of everything else, and it was nearly midnight, he'd be just coming off his shift.

Very vaguely, I remember her leaving and assuring my grandfather she could drive perfectly well by herself, she often did. Then almost as though it was part of a dream, I heard my grandfather speaking on the telephone to my mother, calling her Ingeborg, telling her that I'd come for a visit, and something had disagreed with me so I'd better stay the night.

"Just something he ate," I heard him say. "He'll be fine tomorrow."

I felt him cover me, and put a pillow under my head.

10

My grandfather woke me at quarter to six the next morning. I was due at Sweet Mouth in an hour and forty-five minutes. I'd slept in my clothes, including my new cashmere sweater. My grandfather lent me one of his shirts, and I took a shower while he made us bacon and eggs and squeezed fresh oranges. He was talking on the telephone to someone named Verner when I came out of the bathroom. I heard him say his grandson was visiting him. He really sounded pleased.

We had breakfast and watched the sun come up, sitting on his screened-in patio, overlooking the ocean. He was playing an opera called *Louise*.

"It's worth getting up early to see such a beautiful sight," he said as he watched the sunrise. He was wearing white silk pajamas and a black silk robe.

I began gulping down the orange juice.

"Thirsty from last night's wine?" he said.

Not only that, I had a headache, but I pretended that wasn't it at all and said, "I just never have fresh orange juice. My mother buys Minute Maid."

"Why don't you squeeze the oranges yourself? It tastes better, doesn't it?"

"I don't think we even own an orange-juice squeezer," I complained.

"You can buy one for under a dollar," he said.

"Maybe I will."

He poured me another glass from the pitcher on the table and we ate in silence for a while, watching the sun ease up into the blue beginnings of an early-morning sky.

"Beautiful!" he exclaimed. "Beauty can pierce you like a pain."

I was more interested in something else that was liable to pierce me, like my father's fist.

"Was my mother mad?"

"I think she was shocked to know that you were here."

I groaned and chewed my bacon.

"Why didn't you tell her about coming here the last time?"

"I just didn't."

"Were you afraid to tell her, Buddy?"

"I've been in the doghouse since I met Skye. This wouldn't help."

"I see." He poured himself a cup of coffee.

"I was twenty-three when your mother was born," he said. "Six months later, your grandmother brought her here to America. I hardly knew your grandmother. I was young. I'd gotten her into trouble. I married her."

"It doesn't matter," I said.

"When you got a girl pregnant in those days, you married her."

"Okay," I said.

"What does 'okay' mean?"

"Whatever happened, happened."

"You don't care why?"

"It was a long time ago," I said.

"I had no feeling for your grandmother," he continued. "I didn't feel about her the way you feel about this young lady of yours."

I was shoveling the eggs and bacon in my mouth, embarrassed that he was going into it all. I was my father's son, all right. I didn't know how to talk about personal stuff.

"She was just a girl who wanted to go to America where her own mother already was. I was a boy who loved my home, my homeland."

My grandfather watched the bird feeders for a while. There were chickadees and finches and nuthatches descending on them. There was a cardinal and his wife, and some grackles.

65

"We got drunk one night," he said, "the way you got drunk last night."

"I'm sorry about last night."

"You needn't apologize."

"I never drink, really."

"Not even wine with meals, as you said?"

"A glass maybe, once every six months."

"That's why it took so little," said my grandfather. "And you drank fast."

He filled a pipe with tobacco and watched the birds.

"We got drunk," he said, "and your mother was the result. It's not a pretty story, I'm sorry to say."

"At least it's clearer."

"Then there was the war," he said. A whole flock of titmice swooped down on the feeders. "We didn't even write each other, until she wrote me some four months after she'd arrived in America. She announced that she'd managed to divorce me. I believe it was a vast relief to both of us."

I poured myself the last of the orange juice.

"If your mother had been a boy, I suppose I would have been quicker to trace her after the war. A daughter is always her mother's child, and a son his father's."

"I get along better with my mother," I said.

"Are you more like her or your father?"

"I'm more like him."

"That's what I mean," he said.

He lit his pipe with a gold lighter he took from the pocket of his robe. "After the war I was traveling: Europe, South America, Cuba . . . *Cuba*. I was thirty-seven when I met Carla."

"You were thirty-seven before you ever fell in love?"

"I think until then I was in love only with myself."

I laughed, and he smiled and took a sip of his coffee.

"Life might have been different if I'd met her earlier," he said, "but then regrets are the natural property of gray hairs." He looked at a gold watch he had placed in front of him on the table. "Do you have a driver's license, Buddy?"

"I have my junior's."

"Do you want to drive my jeep in to work?"

"You're kidding?" I said. "By myself?"

"I'm lazy." He laughed. Then he looked across the table at me thoughtfully for some seconds before he said, "You're lazy, too, Buddy. If you're going to drink wine, you should learn how to drink it and how to pour it. If you want fresh orange juice in the morning, you should squeeze it for yourself and not blame your mother because she has only Minute Maid. You should learn about opera, and that a lady always has to be escorted home after a date . . . and you should always own up to where you've been."

"Look, Grandpa!" I said, pointing at some strange black-and-white birds with tufted red heads.

"Those are pileated woodpeckers," he said. Then he laughed again. "And Buddy," he said, "you should never point at anything but French pastries."

Kick worked Sundays, so he was never in Sweet Mouth on Mondays. I watched the clock, waiting for it to be ten so I could call Skye, and shot the bull with Ollie, who nursed a Coke for about an hour and a half. Ollie said he hated summer because he was nothing in summer, but when school started he was a football hero again. I pretended I was anxious to get summer over with, too, but Ollie didn't believe me because he sensed something big was happening to me. He said we didn't have the same rapport anymore. I said for God's sake, don't *you* start making me feel guilty. I'd turn into a big blob of guilt by the time September rolled around if everybody didn't just get off my back, and Ollie said my nose would be so far out of joint by then I wouldn't be good enough for anyone, anyway. He said his mother said the Penningtons were swimming in money from all the oil wells they owned and probably choking on their caviar over the idea of their daughter dating me. He said it didn't matter how handsome I was. According to his mother it wasn't what you looked like in that crowd, it was who you were. I said thanks a lot for telling me his mother's opinions —it made my day—and I carried off his half-empty Coke while he threatened to clobber me.

At ten o'clock I called Skye.

"I got home okay," she said. "Don't worry about it. How are *you*?" she said, not waiting for my answer. "Oh, Buddy, this has been a perfect day because I got the news that I've been accepted at Bryn Mawr for fall and my grades were never that good in the ninth place! I'm really thrilled, Buddy, because originally I wanted to be a Cliffie, go to Radcliffe, but they'd never let me in there, they're grinds, and now it doesn't matter!"

"Fantastic!" I said, with my heart sinking to my shoes. One thing we'd never discussed was our age difference. We both knew we had one but we never talked about it. I knew Connie Spreckles was only a year older than I was, and I knew Skye had been eighteen for only a few months before I met her, so I counted on the fact it wasn't that important. But I felt really creepy hearing she was going to college in the fall and I'd be heading back to Seaville High for another year. . . . I also felt desperate and determined to live that summer like it was the last one of my life.

She asked me to come by when I finished work and I said it'd probably be later (after my father broke every bone in my body, I thought to myself), and I told her I'd call her.

"I want to celebrate!" she said. "I want to do something subtle!"

"We'll do something beautiful," I said. "Beauty can pierce you like a pain."

"What did you just say?" she said.

"Beauty can pierce you like a pain," I said.

"Oh, Buddy!" she said. "What a super thing to say!"

When I came out of Kick's office, my mother was standing there.

I took a break and we left Sweet Mouth and walked down to the A&P parking lot where she'd left the Toyota. I got in and she got in, and she said she couldn't stay in town long because she'd left Streaker with my father, who wasn't in any mood to baby-sit that morning.

"How did you get to work?" she said.

"Grandpa Trenker loaned me his jeep."

"*You're* driving *his* jeep?"

"I had to get here from Montauk somehow!"

"Oh, Buddy," she said.

"Is there anything wrong with my seeing my own grandfather?" I said.

"He's your grandfather in name only," she said. "He's not your grandfather. What did he ever do that made him your grandfather?"

"He had you," I said.

"He had me, all right, up to *here*," she said, drawing her finger across her neck. "He didn't want to know from me all through my childhood!"

"He told me the whole story," I said.

"*His* version of the whole story," she said.

"It made sense," I said.

"Oh did it?" she said. "Did it make sense that my mother worked her fingers to the bone to raise me without one bit of support from him? My mother dropped dead of a heart attack when she was forty-nine because she never had any help from anyone bringing up a child in a strange country, Buddy!"

"She divorced Grandpa, Mom, when you were a baby!"

"And that let him off the hook?"

"When you divorce somebody you divorce somebody, don't you? Ollie's mother's raising him by herself."

"And look at Ollie!" my mother said. "He's fat and he's lonely and Helen Kidd has turned into a vicious gossip because she's so miserable!"

"Mom," I said, "I can understand if you're on the outs with Grandpa Trenker, but he didn't do anything to me. He's done only nice things for me."

"Well aren't you the lucky one, Buddy!"

"I could learn a lot from Grandpa Trenker," I said.

"Yes, I'm sure. You could learn to be a big snotnose from Grandpa Trenker!" I'd never heard my mother say a word like that, and if Streaker or I had said it, we'd have gotten a swat from her we'd feel for days.

"There's nothing wrong with knowing about things,"

69

I said. "I'm not going to learn about things from you and Dad."

"What things aren't you going to learn about from me and Dad?"

"Things," I said.

"What things?" she demanded.

"Ways of the world," I said. "Opera, birds, wine— I don't know."

"Did you say wine?" she said.

"Not wine," I said. "How to pour wine."

"I know how to pour wine and so does your father. You take the top off the bottle and pour it! What are you even *talking* about, Buddy Boyle?"

"I can't explain it to you," I said. "You won't understand. But I don't know how to act around certain people! I feel like a creep around certain people! I go to Beauregard and I feel like a creep because I don't know how to act, or what to say, or anything!"

"I told you that you were in over your head with that girl! It's that girl!"

"Mom," I said, and I was trying to fight back tears that were coming, "I love that girl!" I'd never said anything like that to her or my father. "Am I supposed to just walk away from her because I don't know about things she knows about and all her friends know about?"

My mother stared at me, and her eyes softened suddenly, and she looked like she was going to bawl, too.

"You're too young to be in love, Buddy," she said quietly.

"What age do you have to be?" I said.

"Oh, Buddy," and the tears started rolling down her cheeks.

"I want to know about things," I said. I was bawling, too, right there in the A&P parking lot, trying to hide it with the back of my hand.

My mother took some Kleenex out of her bag and passed me one.

"Thanks," I said.

"I was at this dinner party in Lefrak City once and I didn't even know what fork to pick up," she said, "and I never forgot it. I still wouldn't know. I see what you mean, Buddy, don't think I don't see, but those are snob things and your father and I aren't raising you to think those things are important."

"You're not raising me to think those things are important because you don't know about those things," I said. "You couldn't raise me that way if you wanted to, because you don't know."

"Grandpa Trenker knows all about those things, I suppose," my mother said. "That's his speed all right!"

"Mom," I said, "he's not a bad man. He might have been a lousy father but he's a nice man."

"Your father says maybe you should just go and live with Grandpa Trenker if you're so impressed with him."

"I didn't say I was impressed with him, did I? I said I like him."

"You took that girl out there, didn't you, so you could impress *her* with a fancy relative?"

"Mom," I said, "this isn't getting us anywhere, and I have to go back to work. I left one guy handling the whole floor and it's almost noon."

"Are you coming home after work?" she said.

"What's Dad's mood like?"

"It's not good, Buddy. He says he doesn't care if he ever sees your face again."

"Then maybe he won't," I said, and I pushed down on the door handle.

"Come home after work," she said. "I'll talk to your father."

I blew my nose and stuck the Kleenex in my pocket. "Tell him I don't look forward to being beat up in the backyard again," I said.

"Buddy, he just doesn't know how to handle this. Neither do I."

"I'll handle it myself, Mom," I said. "I've been lazy about handling my problems, but I'm not going to be anymore."

"Come home after work," she said.

"I'll be there after he's gone," I said. I had to get my clothes, anyway.

71

11

I'd been living at my grandfather's for four days. For the first time in my life, I had my own room, with an ocean view. Every morning I drove the jeep to work, and after work I headed over for a swim in the pool with Skye.

On the Friday of the Fourth of July weekend, as I was on my way to Beauregard, I heard a police siren behind me. I pulled over and looked at my father through the rearview mirror, sauntering up toward the jeep with his policeman's cap pushed back on his head, one hand in his pocket. It was our first encounter since the one in the backyard when he'd clobbered me with his fist.

"How you doing?" he said.

"Okay."

There was this little smile playing on his lips, and he couldn't look at me while he talked to me. He watched the road ahead and lit a cigarette.

"How do you like being on your own?"

"I like it fine."

"I can see why," he said, giving the jeep door a slap with his hand, grinning more. He took a puff on his cigarette and we didn't say anything for a while.

"How's Streaker?" I said.

"He's a great kid," my father said. The day I'd packed and cleared out, Streaker wouldn't come down from a tree in our front yard. I'd stood under the tree and tried to talk to him, tried to explain I had to take care of my problems, and he had to learn to fend for himself until I got myself straightened out.

"I don't want your stupid catcher's mitt," he'd said.

"Good!" I'd said. "I can still use it."

72

Then I'd said, "Aren't you going to come down for a good-bye hug?"

"I don't hug," he'd said. "I'm not a girl."

"I can see that," I'd said. "You're a cat that's been treed. Well, meow, Streaker. Thanks for being so understanding."

"I don't care if I never see your face again," he'd said.

"You're not a cat at all," I'd said. "You're the family parrot, parroting everything Dad says."

"Go to hell!" he'd yelled after me, and I'd walked toward Fireplace Road carrying my duffel bag, getting ready to hitch a ride to Montauk.

My father took a couple more drags on his cigarette and I sat in the jeep watching his face in profile. He wasn't in a bad mood. I think he really wanted to talk to me.

"You don't drive this thing after nine at night, do you?" he said.

"Of course not," I said. "Grandpa Trenker wouldn't let me if I wanted to."

"I don't know anything about your grandfather Trenker," he said.

"He's a nice guy," I said.

"I'm not concerned with *him*," he said.

"I'm doing okay," I said.

"I can see that," said my father.

"You been going clamming?" I asked.

"I'm going to take my boy clamming tomorrow," he said, as though he had only one boy.

"Have a nice time," I said. "I hope you and your boy get a big haul."

"Okay, Buddy," he sighed. "I've got to get back on duty."

"Duty calls," I said.

"How would you know?" he said.

"Have you said what you want to say?" I asked him.

"Don't let me keep you" was his answer, and he gave me this little wave and walked back to the police car.

73

I waited for him to turn around and head the other way, and then I went on to Beauregard.

It put me in a really bad mood, which I'd been veering toward all day because Skye was going to another dance at The Hadefield that night, and I wasn't invited. Skye said it was a members-only thing, and she had to go because her brother was just back from Europe. The family had reserved a table; it was the annual Fourth of July Dance.

When I got to Beauregard, her brother was there with some friend he'd traveled through Europe with, this shrimp who came up to my shoulder, named Lennie Waterhouse.

I shook hands with Og first and Lennie second.

Og was tall like his father, with black hair like Skye's and the same green eyes. Mrs. Pennington called him "Junior" and waddled around after him, down by the pool, while Lennie sat in one of the blue-and-white director's chairs and read a paperback Agatha Christie.

"Lennie is going to Princeton next year," Skye told me while we clung to the float in the center of the pool. "He's going to be an art historian."

I didn't ask her what an art historian was, but in the next breath she gave me an idea. "Someday he'll be the director of a big museum. I just love art, particularly anything to do with Renaissance art, which is going to be Lennie's specialty. I could spend an eternity in Rome. We were there two summers ago for a month and I didn't even care that it was so hot you could fry an egg on the Via Veneto."

"What's your brother going to be?" I changed the subject.

"When he finishes Yale, he's going to be a nepotist," she said.

"A *what*?"

"He's going to join Penn Industries," she said. "He's going to work for Daddy."

"What does a nepotist do exactly?" I said.

"A nepotist works for his daddy, or his uncle or his aunt," she laughed. "Nepotism is the fine old art of finding a job through a relative."

"That's a new one on me," I said.

"I like that, Buddy," she said, and she was looking at me again that way she had of looking at me, with her eyes fixed right on mine. "I like showing you things. Do you like me to show you things?"

"I don't know." I had to look away.

"Swim to the bottom of the pool with me and I'll show you some things," she said, and she dove under the float. I followed her. We held our breaths as long as we could, touched lips, she put her hands in my hair, and we surfaced, laughing.

We were winded, and hung on the float, the late-afternoon sun in our eyes. She reached for my hand. "You're rare, Buddy," she said. "Do you think I am?"

"You're more medium," I said, "or well done," and she splashed me and swam away, until I finally caught her by the legs near the pool ladder. We climbed out and dried off, and Skye picked her watch up from the table and said, "It's five o'clock! I've got to get a firecracker under me if I'm going to be beautiful tonight, even though I don't care whether I'm beautiful tonight or not, because you're not going to be there. Maybe I'll be dowdy, instead, and Lennie and Og can pretend they didn't come with me."

"Lennie?" I said. "Is Lennie a member of The Hadefield, too? I thought he was from Michigan?"

"He's our guest, Buddy."

"I didn't know you could take guests," I said.

"He's from out of town, Buddy. I mean, we can't just all prance off to the club and tell him to scramble himself some eggs or something."

"I don't care," I said.

"I think you do," she said. "You sound like you do, but honestly, Buddy, you can't expect us to leave him home when he's our guest for the weekend." She put her towel around my neck and pulled me toward her. "I think you're actually jealous, Buddy. I think I like that."

"I am, a little," I admitted.

"Be jealous a lot, Buddy, not a little," she whispered to me. "I want you to feel a lot toward me, not a little."

"I do," I said, I *croaked*, because she was getting to me, we were so close we were practically kissing, and she whispered, "Me, too."

When I got back to Montauk around six thirty, my grandfather's Alfa Romeo wasn't in the driveway. I parked the jeep and took the long steps leading down to the ocean, and walked around on the beach for a while. I'd told my grandfather I'd be there for dinner with him that night, and I figured he was probably out shopping. On weekends he liked to drive into Amagansett to shop at the Gristede's market just outside the town. He liked to go in the early evening when it wasn't crowded with summer people.

I walked around for a while on the hard sand near the surf and thought about Skye, which I was doing nonstop, all the time, anyway. I'd never been in a situation that didn't have a future, the way Skye and I didn't. I'd never even thought seriously of a future with a girl, beyond some dumb high-school dance coming up in a few months, or a game, or a party. Even though I tried to tell myself to just make the most of the time we did have together that summer, my mind ached and my body yearned when I tried to imagine fall without her. How was I going to go back to the Seaville girls after Skye? How the *hell*, as my father would put it, was I going to get along without Skye? Bryn Mawr was way off somewhere in Pennsylvania, and I was on the tip of Long Island. I'd be a senior in some hick high school and she'd be a freshman in this fancy college. Even if I could hitchhike across three states to see her, I'd be competing with the Lennie Waterhouses of the world, and I didn't even know what Renaissance art was! . . . Then I got steamed all over again at the idea of Lennie being invited to the dance at the club when I wasn't. I had a feeling she wasn't telling me the truth about The Hadefield Club affairs. I didn't know how anybody at The Hadefield could tell whether I was a weekend guest of theirs or not, and it seemed to me I could have been sneaked in somehow, if the Penningtons had wanted me to go.

76

All of this was churning through my mind and my stomach as I made my way back toward the steps leading up to my grandfather's. For a moment I saw the little white car parked at a cut in the beach without really registering it. There was elephant grass obscuring it, but it was plainly a Fiat convertible, and as I took that information in very slowly, and turned around for another look, I saw him very clearly. I saw the yellow glasses, and I saw the binoculars he was holding, and I saw the direction they were aimed in: up. He was watching my grandfather's house.

I don't know if he saw me. The steps I was starting up were around the side of the cliff, so I doubted it. When I was walking along the beach, he might have focused on me.

I wondered if he was a bird-watcher. The feeders at my grandfather's attracted every kind of bird there was anywhere near the shore.

I planned to tell my grandfather about it, but when I reached the top of the steps, my grandfather came running out, calling at me that *she* would be there any minute, that I'd better shower and change fast!

"Who?" I said. "What are you talking about?"

"Didn't you read the note I left on the table?"

"I didn't go in the house," I said.

He put his arm around my shoulder and practically trotted me along the rest of the way. He said, "In about ten minutes your mother is arriving for dinner."

12

My grandfather did everything well, including cook.
He served us a filet of fish in spinach with shrimp and
mushrooms, and a salad of fresh bean sprouts from his
garden. In the center of the table he put a bouquet of
red and pink roses he'd cut from the vines outside the
patio. We all had a glass of wine with the meal, and
instead of opera playing on the tape he had Strauss
waltzes.

It took a while for my mother to unbend. My mother
always wore pantsuits in the summer when she went
out with my father, but that night she was in one of
her best dresses, the kind she wore to Mass Sundays. It
was a light blue dress, shades lighter than her eyes,
and she had on white heels, carried a white bag, and
wore her best earrings which were gold with pearls in
the center. She looked really nice, a lot more dressed
up than my grandfather and me. She wasn't saying
much to either of us in the beginning. I think she said
more to Mignon, carrying on one of those conversations like: "Well aren't you a nice dog. . . . She says,
'Yes, I *am*.' . . . You have a lot of hair in your eyes,
Mignon. . . . She says, 'I can hardly see out.'" That
sort of thing, before we all sat down at the table.

My grandfather did most of the talking, at first. He
told her how much he'd traveled before he'd finally
settled in Montauk, naming all the countries he'd been
in, and elaborating on how much it meant to him to
finally have roots.

"What is it exactly you did?" my mother asked him.

"Bitte?" he said. "What do you mean?"

My mother shrugged her shoulders. "For a living?"

"Ah! Yes! I was an art dealer, a dealer in gold coins,

78

rare stamps. I did whatever I could. *Wer rastet, rostet.*"
He chuckled.

"I never learned German," said my mother. "I picked
some up from Mommy. Very little, though, because
Mommy wanted to be a real American, and she wanted
me to be one, too. We never spoke German together."

"Wer rastet, rostet means who rests, rusts." My
grandfather chuckled again. "Now I'm resting and rust-
ing. Oh, I rarely buy or sell art anymore."

"I would like to know something about Renaissance
art," I said. "Did you ever hear of that?"

"Yes I heard of that," said my grandfather.

"That's a new one on me," my mother said, "Buddy
wanting to know about art."

"Renaissance art," I said.

"That's a new one on me, you wanting to know
about any kind of art."

"The *Lorelei* inspires the interest," my grandfather
said.

"The what?"—my mother.

"The girl. Am I right, Buddy?"

"Oh *her*. Well I've had her up to here," my mother
said, drawing her finger across her neck.

"Renaissance art was developed first and most fully
in Italy," said my grandfather. "Florence was the great
center of the Renaissance masters. You've heard of
Michelangelo, Buddy, and Leonardo da Vinci. Giotto?
Fra Angelico?"

"Some of them I've heard of," I said. "Michelangelo
and da Vinci."

"I'll go into it with you," my grandfather promised.
"I have many books for you to study, if you'd like to."

"Why did you settle here?" my mother asked. "How
come you didn't go back to Germany?"

"Where I lived is East Germany now," said my
grandfather. "I could not live with the Communists. To
quote one of your own famous statesmen, 'Communism
is the death of the soul.' Do you remember Adlai
Stevenson, Buddy? It was he who said that when he
was accepting his nomination in nineteen fifty-two."

"I've heard of him," I said.

"I remember him," my mother said. "He was a liberal."

"Not that liberal," my grandfather said, "not like some who played into the hands of the Communists."

"We had a red out here one summer just down the street from us, a summer renter," my mother said. "If he wasn't a real red, he was a pinko. He was against the war in Vietnam and you name it. Bill used to come home from down there boiling!"

"It wasn't a good war," I said.

"Our boys were fighting in that war!" my mother said.

"It still wasn't a good war!" I said.

"Oh no war is a good war," said my grandfather.

"Well if our boys are in it, I say support our boys. One thing I am is loyal to my own," said my mother. She looked sorry that she'd said it and went on quickly, with flushed cheeks. "I'd tell Bill, don't go down there and drink with him because you just come home with your motor running!"

"Is Dad off tonight?" I said, to change the subject.

"He took Streaker to see *Bambi*. He borrowed Rob Hayden's car, so I could take the Toyota. I've seen *Bambi* three times. Bill says to me, after *you* called"—she glanced across at my grandfather (she was starting to feel her second glass of wine)—"'so go out and have dinner with them, it won't kill you' and . . ." her voice trailed off.

"I'm delighted that you came," said my grandfather.

For the first time my mother gave him a little smile. "I'm not sorry myself."

"Good!" my grandfather said. "Would you like another helping?"

"I don't mind if I do," my mother said. "I usually fry flounder. Bill's always coming home with some he's caught or Rob's caught, and I just stick it in the pan, because Bill would practically let me fry good steak, he's so nuts about anything fried."

I don't exactly remember how it got started, but a short while after dinner my mother mentioned some German song her mother sang, and my grandfather said,

"Ah *'Muss i 'denn'!'*" and before I knew it they were singing softly together, my mother's face soft and relaxed, and my grandfather's eyes shining.

It was Mignon who interrupted the singing. She began barking very loudly way down behind the house. My grandfather called her, but she wouldn't come and she wouldn't stop barking.

"I'd better go see what's bothering her," said my grandfather, and for the first time that evening I remembered De Lucca parked down on the beach.

I didn't have time to mention it to my grandfather because he just took off after Mignon, but in a while, I heard him calling me.

"Bring me a heavy towel from the bathroom, Buddy, and my gloves!" he shouted up to me. "It's a trapped animal!"

"Oh *no!*" my mother exclaimed, and I got the towel and the gloves.

"Turn on the outside lights!" my grandfather shouted. "Bring the flashlight!"

My mother ran after me, down the path behind the house. Mignon was whining then, and dancing around where my grandfather was kneeling. I turned the flashlight on the face of a small raccoon my grandfather was freeing from a steel trap.

My grandfather put on the gloves and lifted the bleeding creature from the jaws of the thing, saying, "Now you'll be all right, *Liebchen.*"

The raccoon actually had tears of pain in his eyes, and my grandfather wrapped the towel around him.

"Oh my God!" my mother said. "The poor little thing."

"My neighbor is protecting his precious garbage!" my grandfather said bitterly.

He carried the raccoon back in his arms, telling me as we went, "I want you to call 324–2455 when we get inside. You'll be talking to Dr. Baird in East Hampton. Explain what happened and tell him I am bringing the animal to him. I'm sorry we have to end the evening this way, Ingeborg."

81

"I could take him to the doctor on my way back to Seaville," said my mother.

"You can't drive and hold him," said my grandfather. "He's in pain, and terrified."

"I'll go with her, Grandfather," I said. "We can do it together, and I'll sleep home tonight."

"Then tell the doctor I'll come in the morning for him," my grandfather said. "You'll wear these gloves, and hold him in the towel."

When we were ready to leave, my grandfather walked us down to the Toyota. "Nothing is so cruel as the steel trap," he said. "I saw a mother raccoon die tearing herself to pieces to reach starving young, and a baby raccoon caught in a trap like that being gnawed and pulled apart by drooling dogs."

"Don't," my mother said.

"I'm sorry, Ingeborg. I hate those traps. They should be outlawed. What woman can wear fur from a fox that slowly froze to death? For someone's vanity, animals are tortured! Is he doing all right, Buddy?"

"Yes, we'll take good care of him."

On the way home from the doctor's my mother said, "Well, he couldn't be all bad. He has a heart, Buddy, I'll give him that."

"I'll give him a lot more than that," I said.

"Buddy," my mother said, "your father and I had a talk. We want to start all over with this thing."

"Meaning what?" I said.

"Meaning let's just forget the past. Bygones are bygones."

"What about Grandfather Trenker?"

"I said 'bygones are bygones,'" she said. "I'm not going to fall all over him and call him 'Daddy,' but the past is the past."

"I like staying at Grandfather's," I said.

"You like having a jeep to ride around in."

"It's not *just* that."

"I know it's not just that," she said. "I heard all about this thing with Renestence art—"

"Renaissance," I said.

"This art you want to know about," she said. "I get the picture, Buddy, and I told your father it's not as if he wants to smoke pot or drink liquor the way some boys his age do. I said he's in love with this girl who's very high class and he wants to know about things."

"What did Dad say?"

"You know your father, he didn't say that much, but he's not going to stand in your way."

"Thanks for talking to him, Mom," I said.

"Well there's one thing your father will never have to buy me after this evening," said my mother, "and that's a fur coat!"

Later, I played Man on the Mountain with Streaker in our room, in our bunk bed, and my father stood in the doorway for a while and watched us for a second or so. He had that little half-smile he gets on his mouth, but he didn't say much, just to keep it down because we were drowning out the T.V.

"Are you still in trouble?" Streaker whispered to me while I pulled him down by the legs from the top bunk.

"I think it's going to be okay," I said.

That night it looked that way.

13

We named the baby raccoon Graham Cracker, since that was his favorite food. He ate Mignon's dry dog food, too, and Mignon tolerated this and even let Graham examine the hair on her head, searching through it as though he was looking for Mignon's eyes.

Dr. Baird had bandaged Graham's hind leg and given him shots, and my grandfather had built him a large cage we kept in the backyard. A lot of the time we brought Graham inside and gave him the run of the house, but he was still timid and new to people, and he spent much of his time high on the rafters of my grandfather's cathedral living-room ceiling, peering down at us through his tiny masked eyes.

My grandfather had an argument with his neighbor over the steel trap. He'd told his neighbor he would systematically search for any the neighbor put out and confiscate them, and the neighbor had threatened to bill him for them.

That Fourth of July weekend, when I wasn't working, I spent most of my time in Montauk. Skye kept making excuses for why she couldn't see me. It was a family weekend, she said; she said we had the whole summer, but just that weekend she would have to stay at Beauregard and help entertain their many guests. In the next breath she'd tell me that she and Og and Lennie had smoked pot down at the dunes and watched the sun come up, adding always in her coy way that she'd missed me, thought of me all the time, particularly after the pot because pot made you horny.

"A woman teases that way," said my grandfather. "You can play that game, too, Buddy. Tell her you have things to do as well, and when she's ready finally to see you, make a date a day later."

I could really talk to him about her, and we spent a lot of time discussing things. When I showed him the new clothes I'd bought, he told me I'd gone overboard, and not selected things carefully. Quality, he advised, is better than quantity. One very good belt on a pair of old jeans is better than three pairs of new jeans and a cheap belt.

"Less is always more," he said, "in everything."

"I don't exactly know what that means."

"One long-stemmed white rose is better than a whole bouquet of carnations," he said. "If you don't know many operas, learn one very well. If you want to speak about Renaissance art, as you seem to want to, select one artist—Botticelli, for example—he was a master of color and rhythmic line. Learn all you can about just Sandro Botticelli."

"I think I understand," I said.

"Sometime soon stop calling yourself 'Buddy,' too," my grandfather said. "Buddy is a boy's name, not a man's."

"That would make two Bills in our family," I said.

"Don't you have a middle name?"

"It's Raymond," I complained.

"Raymond is better than Buddy," he said.

I said, "I don't exactly see how I can just become Raymond around here overnight."

"You can become anything you want to be," said my grandfather. "It's a matter of authority. Whatever a man's confidence, that's his capacity."

"That sounds good, Grandpa Trenker," I said, "but I don't have that much confidence."

"Confidence isn't something you're born with, Buddy, and it isn't something that comes down on you one day like the rain. You get it for yourself, gradually, willfully, and it's the best gift you can give yourself."

I knew what Grandfather meant, but on the last night of that long weekend when Skye called to ask me by the next day, I became living proof of the old saying you can't make a silk purse out of a sow's ear. Instead

85

of making a date a day later, I said I'd be at Beauregard an hour earlier than the one she'd suggested.

When I got to work that morning, Mrs. Townsend was there before me. No one in Seaville called her Mrs. Richards, even though she'd been married to Kick for five years. She's a woman in her fifties, tiny, with this little bird's face and these short, thin bird's legs, and she was fluttering around in his office, opening drawers and throwing papers around, in a tirade about his pot-smoking.

"He was a brilliant actor once," she said to no one in particular (although I was the only one around: the cook was in the kitchen), "and now he's literally gone to pot! He's wasted! He's a waste! . . . That goes and so does that!" She threw some Easy Wider cigarette papers into the wastebasket, along with a roach clip. "And this goes!" She threw a small bag of pot in on top of the rest. "He sleeps fourteen hours a day!" she said.

I didn't say anything. I just hoped I'd be off duty by the time Kick showed up at Sweet Mouth, which I was.

The rain was really coming down by the time I was finished work that afternoon. I stopped at the A&P to get another box of crackers for Graham, along with more sunflower seeds and some marshmallows, and I met Ollie as I was coming out.

"Do you want to go to the movies tonight?" he asked me.

"I think I have a date," I said.

"We could double because I'm taking LuAnn Derby."

"You won't like the movies with LuAnn," I said. "She talks all through the movies."

"So do I," he said. "What do you do, *listen* to all that crap in the movies? Movies, Buddy-wuddy, are to talk in and eat popcorn in." He laughed very hard at his own joke and slapped my back so hard I almost dropped my bag of groceries.

"I'm not going to be Buddy anymore," I said. "I'm going to start calling myself Ray. Got it?"

"Ray?"

"Ray," I said.

"Fine with me, Ray," he said. "I'll see you around, Ray."

"See you around," I said. I started walking toward the parking lot when he called out, "Hey, Ray?"

"What?"

The rain was teeming down and the bag of groceries was turning a wet brown.

"I'm not going to be Ollie anymore," he said. "I'm going to start calling myself Gertrude. Got it?" Then he raised his pant leg, flung his ankle back, and howled.

Og and Lennie Waterhouse were just pulling out in Og's Mercedes as I drove through the gates at Beauregard. We exchanged honks, and I parked as near the front door as I could, then waited for Peacock to let me in.

Skye answered the door, all in light brown that afternoon.

"It's Peacock's day off," she said. "Guess what? We're alone, Buddy!"

I didn't show her what I had with me until we went into the solarium on the first floor, and she turned on a tape of punk rock.

She clapped her hands together when she saw it. "Grass!" she said. "Where'd you get it?"

I'd fished it out of the wastebasket at Sweet Mouth before I'd gone off duty.

She didn't wait to hear where I'd gotten it. She ran off to get some cigarette paper up in Og's room, exclaiming as she went that it was the perfect thing to do on a rainy afternoon.

I'd never had much experience with grass beyond a drag once or twice when it was being passed around at a party. I'd never sat down to have grass with anyone because no one I knew was into it. If I thought what happened out in the backyard a while before between my father and me was bad, I'm here to tell you I'd have had bigger surprises, like some broken bones, if my father knew I had anything to do with marijuana.

My father said the word marijuana the way someone else would say "filthy!" He could arrest ten drunken drivers in a week's time and laugh it off saying this one had a load on or that one was seeing double, but if he made one arrest where he found marijuana on the "perpetrator" (that's his favorite word—"perpetrator") he'd act like he'd had dealings with a child molester. I never mentioned the fact Kick smoked because my father would have swooped down on Sweet Mouth and made an arrest before you could say "controlled substance," which was a police synonym for the weed. My dad knew there was smoking going on at Seaville High —name me a high school where there isn't some of it going on—but he just trusted I'd never get involved with it. He'd never even said I shouldn't; he just took it for granted no one named William Raymond Boyle, Jr., would take the chance of turning on and meeting death at the hands of his own father.

"This is a really neat surprise," Skye said while she rolled some. "What gave you the idea, Buddy?"

"Do you think Og and Lennie are the only pair who've ever smoked pot?" I said. "Why is it such a big deal?" I shrugged my shoulders and pretended I always went around with a bag of pot in my pants pocket.

"I just never knew *you* were into it," Skye said.

"Why? Because I don't go to college?" I laughed.

When Skye lit the joint and inhaled, she said, "Hey, this is strong stuff, Buddy. We only need a half joint for now."

I took a drag and coughed, and Skye said, "You don't hold it in your lungs. You won't feel it if you don't hold it in."

She took another drag, and I did, holding it in, and we listened to the punk rock. It was an old group and you couldn't even make out what they were singing. We finished nearly all of the cigarette before long.

"Do you believe in interplanetary travel, Buddy?"

"Is that when two people do this?" I said, reaching for her, and she said, "Oh Buddy, that isn't subtle at all, there's nobody home."

"What does *that* mean?"

"That means that's kid stuff, Buddy, trying to make out because Daddy and Mommy are gone and *whoosh-bang* the door is shut and you're alone and you start trying to make out!"

"*Whoosh-bang* the door is shut?" I said. It seemed hilarious, and I sank my shoulders into the soft couch and held my sides laughing.

"*Whoosh-bang* the door is shut!" Skye said, and laughed, too.

"*Whoosh-dang* the bore is shut," I said.

"Are you the bore?"

"I'm the bore," I said. "I'm shut."

"I'm glut," she said. "I'm hungry."

"I'm butt," I said. "Sit on me."

"I'm slut," she said. "I run around a lot."

"I'm Tut," I said. "I'm a king."

"I'm rut," she said, "and you're in me."

"I'm cut," I said, "and I'm open."

"I'm mutt," she said. "*Bowwow.*"

Then I told her about Graham and how great my grandfather had been, and she listened and I went on and on about him, my grandfather, not Graham, and she said she had a secret but first she wanted to talk about interplanetary travel.

"Is that when two people do this?" I said, reaching for her, and for a while we kissed and began to get involved, with that punk rock roaring behind us, and the rain needling the windows. I could have kept going even though I never had, I knew I could have and it would be all right.

She stopped it. "*Whoosh-bang* the door is shut," she said.

"So what?"

"I have to change the tape and you're not letting me talk about interplanetary travel."

"Go right ahead," I said.

"You don't really want to hear, though."

"I do," I said.

She put on another tape, came back to me, and said,

"The thing I want to say about interplanetary travel is . . ."

"Yes?"

"Is that it's when two people do this," she said, only she wasn't laughing, and we touched each other's faces for the longest time, and held each other. "I don't care about interplanet, inter*plan*,ne,tary, travel," she said. We did fantastic things with our mouths then and she was so light on me, and we stayed very close together, moving so gently. I said I loved her and she said it back, and I almost felt like crying it was so good.

I don't know how many years later she said, "Oh oh, Mummy's back. I hear the car," but it must have been long enough for me to grow to thirty because I didn't feel at all like a kid anymore.

"She's back!" Skye said. "Pocket the roach." I put the small butt into my pocket while she sprayed the solarium with a Listerine breath spray. Then she grabbed my hand and said, "The living room! We were in the living room!" She snapped off the tape and we ran down the marble hallways to the living room.

Skye tossed some magazines on the floor, snapped on the T.V. and kicked off her shoes.

I went across the room and sank into a large armchair.

"Talk," Skye said. The T.V. was playing in the background, too softly for us to hear.

"I'm a hut and natives live in me," I said.

"Talk seriously, or Mummy will know we were up to something."

Then she said, "I'm a putt and I'm on the golf course."

We both laughed. We could hear the front door opening, and Mrs. Pennington called out, "Hello?"

"Hello, Mother!"

"Hello, dear!"

"We're in the living room."

"Who's we?"

"Hello, Mrs. Pennington!"

"She's a strut and she's in a parade," Skye whispered.

"Hello, Buddy!" Mrs. Pennington called back.

"Do you need any help, Mummy?"

"She's shut and she's a door," I said.

"We already did that," Skye said. She whispered across the room at me, "I like the way you make me feel, Buddy," even though there was no need to whisper in Beauregard. The rooms were about a half acre apart.

"Tell me the secret. You were going to tell me a secret," I said.

"Mummy told me in strictest confidence not to tell."

"Is it a secret about Botticelli?" I said. "Is it a secret about his mastery of color and rhythmic line?"

She clapped her hands together just the way her mother often did. "Oh Buddy, you say the dearest things sometimes! Sometimes I can't believe what comes out of your mouth!"

"If it isn't a secret about Botticelli," I said, "who is it a secret about?"

"It's a secret about Mr. De Lucca," she said. "I know who he's looking for."

"Who?"

"Gentlehands. Remember? The SS guard at that concentration camp. He was this terrible sadist and he murdered De Lucca's cousin."

"I think I'm too stoned," I said.

"I'll tell you tonight."

"Do you want to come to Montauk?"

"I'd like that, Buddy."

"Come with me now. We can have dinner there."

"If Mummy lets me," she said.

"Oh Mummy will let you."

"I know it," she laughed.

"But maybe you'd miss Og and Lennie?"

"Maybe," she said smiling, "maybe."

We could hear the *tap tap* of high heels on the marble floor as Mrs. Pennington came toward us.

"*Whoosh-bang* the door is open," I said.

"Mummy," Skye said when Mrs. Pennington entered the living room, "Buddy's asked me to dinner."

The butterfly dogs romped around in polka-dot plastic raincoats. "I wish someone would invite *me* to din-

91

ner," Mrs. Pennington said. "When Peacock's gone, Cook doesn't care *what* we eat because she cooks for him, not *us!* I think she's serving creamed codfish and I abhor codfish! It always tastes like hot cotton and upsets my stomach, which Cook *knows* as well as she knows her name is Cook."

I helped January out of her raincoat while Janice licked my fingers.

"You poor children cooped up on a day like this!" Mrs. Pennington said. "Rain, rain, go a-*way!*"

14

Skye said she wanted to take a bath before she went to Montauk, so I went ahead of her. I was halfway out of Seaville before I realized I was still stoned. I had to keep telling myself where I was and what I was doing. My mind wandered all over the place. I remembered an afternoon in May, after I'd first gotten my learner's permit. I was with my father and Rob Hayden, driving Rob's jeep. We were going fly-casting down at the beach, and they were drinking beer in the back and playing with Rob's CB radio. I kept thinking: they're crazy to let me drive, I don't know what I'm doing, and every time we swooped down over another dune, I felt as though it was a miracle we were still all in one piece. I had the same feeling that rainy afternoon, and just outside Amagansett, I pulled over and tossed the tiny butt of pot I had in my pocket out the window. Then I forced myself to concentrate, and I let the other cars pass me, taking it very slowly until I finally saw my grandfather's driveway with the chain across it.

I told my grandfather Skye was coming for dinner and he said he'd bought some hamburger meat, we could fix something for ourselves, that he was going out for a while on business. He was arranging some wildflowers he'd found on a walk, explaining that they were adder's-tongues, moth mulleins and saxifrages.

"What's the matter with you, Buddy?" he said. "Why are you filling yourself with Wheat Thins when you have a guest for dinner?" I'd eaten almost the whole box, gulping them down by the handful. I'd heard about the appetite pot gives you, and that was probably why I couldn't seem to stop eating the crackers. Graham was grabbing my pant leg, trying to get me to drop a few crackers to him.

"I guess I can tell *you*," I said.

"You guess you can tell me what?"

"I smoked some marijuana with Skye. It makes you really hungry."

He held up the vase and admired the flowers. "Can you still feel it?"

"Not so much now."

"And when you drove from Seaville?"

"*That* was hairy."

He carried the vase over to the table and set it in the center. Graham hopped up to see, and he picked Graham up and stroked him, saying, "Those aren't for you, *Liebchen*."

I hadn't forgotten what Skye had started to tell me about De Lucca. I was going to mention it to my grandfather then. I thought it might explain De Lucca's peering up there that day through binoculars. My grandfather knew many foreigners, one in particular, the man named Verner who called sometimes and spoke German with my grandfather. I didn't think my grandfather liked him because the calls always made him irritated and he complained that Verner had to learn to solve his own problems.

I was about to bring up the subject when my grandfather said, "Opportunity and responsibility go hand in hand, Buddy. Did you ever think of that?"

"I'm not sure what you mean."

"If you have an opportunity to drive a car, you have a responsibility to protect others, and yourself, while you're driving."

"I'll never do it again," I said. "I realized it was wrong the minute I hit the Montauk Highway."

"That was the minute you should have been responsible."

"I know that. I'm sorry."

"Once you know something is wrong, you're responsible, whether you see it, or hear about it, and most particularly when you're a part of it. That's why I'm

94

going to mention something else to you, something I see is wrong."

"All right," I said. He sat down in his armchair and I went over and sat on the couch.

"What are you going to be, Buddy? What do you want to do with your life?"

"I haven't given it a lot of thought," I said.

"Give it a lot of thought," he said. "Those who make the worst use of their time are the first to complain how fast it went." Graham jumped down from his lap and scampered up the drapes to the rafters. "I read somewhere that when you're young you sit like children in a theater before the curtain is raised, in good spirits, eagerly waiting for the play to begin. . . . That is true, I think, but some young people are still sitting there after the curtain rises. They never get to take part. They are the eternal audience, the watchers of other people."

"The way I watch everyone at Beauregard," I said.

"Yes, the way you watch the Penningtons, that's close to what I'm saying. If they are the people you want to be like, you'd better start learning about the things that interest them. Whoever you want to model yourself after, you have to choose and begin."

"I wouldn't mind being like you, Grandpa," I said.

"Thank you, Buddy."

Then he stood up. "I have to be on my way. . . . Buddy, I think you smoked the marijuana today to prove to Skye that you're like her brother and his friend. You're not, you know. You haven't had their advantages. You have a long way to go to catch up to them. Let them cloud their minds and waste their time. You spend your time well and keep your head clear. Don't be a weak person in this life, Buddy, not financially or emotionally or spiritually. You'll be taken advantage of if you are."

"I see what you mean," I said.

"If drugs and liquor weren't so readily available," said my grandfather, "if the poor and the weak could come out of their stupors and see what's being done to them, we'd have riots all over the world."

"Thanks for talking to me about things, Grandfather," I said. "My dad and I don't talk about things much."

"My father and I didn't either," he said. Then he whistled for Mignon. He smiled at me. "Be on stage, Buddy, not in the audience."

Skye and I made hamburgers and played with Graham. We took a long walk down on the beach when the rain stopped, and I made up a lie to impress her and said I'd decided I was going to be a lawyer.

"Uncle Louie says lawyers and painters can soon change white to black," Skye said. "Oh you should hear Uncle Louie on the subject of lawyers! Where are you going to school, Buddy?" I never had to think of an answer to most of her questions because she always went right on. "Go to Haverford for prelaw and then we'll be right next door to each other. Harvard is best for law, of course. You could go there after. Oh, you'd be a Harvard law student, Buddy! Do you know this boy I know named Drake Goode couldn't make Harvard and he's brilliant, too, and Uncle Louie says it's because his name is Goode, not Gold; that the Jews just about run Harvard!"

"Uncle Louie sounds like a really fair man," I said.

"Oh, we're all ashamed of Uncle Louie," Skye said. "Honestly, we hate to go *anyplace* out with him because of the things that come out of his mouth! I went to the ballet with him once and he leaned over and said in this voice everyone for rows in front of us and behind us could hear, 'There's enough fruit up on stage to start a fruit stand!' I could have just died!"

"Do you think we'll see each other when summer's over?" I said.

"I've been thinking about that a lot," she said.

"Well?" I said.

"It'll be tragic if we don't," she said. "I hate and love tragedies, Buddy. I hate them when they happen to me, but I love them when I read them or see them on stage because everything really beautiful that's been written about or set to music is tragic."

96

"That doesn't answer my question," I said.

"Does this?" she said, and she stopped, and pulled me by my slicker until she could put her arms around me. I let her kiss me for a long time and when she stopped, I said, "It still doesn't answer my question."

"An answer is always a form of death," she said. "I read that in *The Magus* by John Fowles. Did you ever read *The Magus,* Buddy? Og used to carry it everywhere with him, and he says it's the most mysterious book he's ever read, including all of Hesse!"

My grandfather was right. I had some catching up to do.

We went back to the house and started the fire my grandfather had laid in the fireplace, and Skye told me it was a good thing she'd left after I did, because she found the bag of pot I'd brought with me, on the table in the solarium.

"I didn't want to carry it here while I was driving," she said. "I'll save it for you. God! I'm glad Mummy didn't see it first!"

"Give it to Og and Lennie," I said. "I don't really turn on that much. . . . You know if drugs and liquor weren't so easy to get, if the poor and the weak could come out of their stupors and see what's being done to them, we'd have riots all over this country!"

"You're deep, Buddy," she said. "At first I didn't think so, I just thought you were this really beautiful number, you know, and my father would say he isn't even out of high school, and I'd say I don't care because I love looking at him, he's better than anything else around here in the summer, but I told Daddy: I didn't know anything about Botticelli when I was a junior. I mean I just had Renaisance Art this semester!"

"What'd Daddy say?" I said.

"Oh Daddy's from the Middle Ages in his mind, he honestly is. He thinks the girl has to be younger than the boy."

We were sitting before the fire talking that way, when my grandfather came in and said not to disturb

97

ourselves, he was just going to have a glass of wine and go somewhere with a good book.

"Don't leave, Mr. Trenker," Skye said. "I was supremely disappointed when you weren't here for dinner. Put on something tragic and we'll all listen to it together, because Buddy and I were just talking a while ago about tragedy."

My grandfather said he'd put on one of his favorite operas, which he hadn't listened to in a long time. He got himself a glass of wine, and we got fresh Cokes, and then Skye began talking nonstop through most of the arias.

She told this long story about how her mother had fallen asleep and begun snoring during a performance of *Boris Godunov*. During Boris' most poignant number, "Farewell, my son, I am dying," someone behind her mother had leaned forward and shook her gently, and her mother had sat bolt upright and cried aloud, "Junior, do you need anything?"

"She'd been nursing my brother though this ghastly attack of bronchitis all that week, and she thought she was home!" Skye said, and we all laughed.

Then suddenly Skye realized my grandfather had put on an opera called *Tosca,* and she sat up and said, "This is the end of *Tosca!*"

My grandfather smiled, and nodded.

"Buddy," she said, "this is the famous aria *O dolci mani* that I was going to tell you about this afternoon."

"We weren't talking about opera this afternoon," I said.

"Well in a way we were," she said. "This is the part when Tosca tells Cavaradossi they are free to go away and love each other. So he's singing '*O dolci mani,*' which translates 'O gentle hands.' That SS officer used to play *Tosca* for all the Jews he guarded, to taunt the ones who were from Rome. It's Puccini, see, and it's set in Rome, and he always sang '*O dolci mani,*' with these horrible trained dogs ready to snarl at anything, right at his feet. So they called him Gentlehands!"

"That's very interesting," my grandfather said. "How did you hear about all this, Skye?"

"A friend of my mother's named Nick De Lucca is —out—here. Oh, Buddy, now I *am* in deep, because I'm not supposed to tell this. I just better shut up right now."

"You can tell Grandpa," I said.

"If it's a confidence, it should remain one," said my grandfather.

"She can tell *you*," I said.

"No, I *shouldn't*," said Skye.

"Don't let anyone convince you to break your word, Skye," said my grandfather.

"I have to go, anyway," Skye said. "It's late."

"Come again," said my grandfather. "It's always a pleasure."

Mignon and I walked Skye out to her Jensen and she was so quiet I finally said, "Well what are you so clammed up about?" and my voice sounded angry, because I had a feeling I knew why she was acting so strangely.

"I can't help it, Buddy, I've got goose bumps."

"I hope you don't think my grandfather is—" I couldn't even finish the sentence.

"When did he come to this country, Buddy?"

"Oh, you're really subtle," I said. "This is really subtle!"

"It's just too big a coincidence for my tiny mind," she said, getting in her car.

"Well, Heil Hitler and good night," I said disgustedly, and I walked away while she was still getting the car started.

15

When I went back inside that night, my grandfather was preparing to fill the bird feeders. He was standing at the kitchen counter. Graham was perched on his shoulder, reaching his paw down for sunflower seeds my grandfather passed up to him.

"We have to let Graham go soon, Buddy."

"How soon?"

"Tomorrow, the next day."

"He still has the bandage on, though."

"If we wait too long, he won't learn to be independent." He turned around and faced me. "I know about De Lucca. I met with him tonight."

"Who is he really looking for?" I asked.

My grandfather shrugged. "This Gentlehands of his."

"Is Gentlehands supposed to be someone *you* know, Grandpa?"

"Mr. De Lucca doesn't think he's someone I know. He thinks that I'm this Gentlehands." My grandfather put his hand on my shoulder. "Don't be alarmed, Buddy. These cases of mistaken identity happen all the time. I was a German during World War Two. This is a fact I've never tried to hide."

"But *could* Gentlehands be someone you know?"

"Who?" my grandfather asked.

"Mr. Verner?"

"Mr. *who?*"

"Verner," I said. "The man who calls here."

"Ah, *him.*" My grandfather chuckled despairingly. "He's no one. He's a very old man who still collects his stamps like a boy."

I told my grandfather about seeing De Lucca that afternoon with the binoculars. I thought he might get angry at me for not mentioning it sooner, but he merely shrugged his shoulders again.

"Let him watch this place. What will he see?"

"What did he say to you tonight?" I said. "Didn't you tell him you had nothing to do with those concentration camps?"

My grandfather picked up the bag of sunflower seeds he'd slit open with his Swiss knife. "He called me and asked to meet with me, and I met with him. How long was I gone? An hour, two? We talked. This Mr. De Lucca is an American of Italian ancestry. He is a newspaperman. It's his business to dig up a lurid story that will sell newspapers. He doesn't care about facts or history or the danger of making libelous insinuations."

"A cousin of his was killed in a concentration camp," I said.

"In Auschwitz, yes. So he said."

"Didn't you tell him you were never anywhere near Auschwitz?"

"A man who listens because he wants to hear that he is right, cannot hear that he is wrong," my grandfather said. "Perhaps that's why this Mr. De Lucca needs his hearing aid."

"Why don't you call the police?"

"What could your father do, for example, if you went to him and said that someone else thought you were a car thief called Hot Hands? Could he make an arrest? Could he stop the maligning of your good name? . . . No. That takes a lawyer, Buddy."

"Are you going to call a lawyer?"

"I may have to," my grandfather said. "Right now I'm going to attend to my birds."

The next morning while I was wrestling with four orders of pancakes and two of eggs over easy, Kick came across to me and told me there was a phone call for me in his office.

"She better mean what she says," he told me. He was in a lousy mood; the rumor around Sweet Mouth was that Mrs. Townsend had told him he had to choose between pot and her.

It was Skye calling.

"What did Kick mean you'd better mean what you said?" I asked her.

"I told him I was arranging for a kiddies' party there, that I was a friend of yours and I wanted to make the arrangements through you."

"There goes my job," I said.

"So I get a dozen towheads from the beach and treat them," Skye said. "I wanted to talk with you, Buddy. I'm sorry about last night."

"My grandfather knows all about De Lucca," I said. "He's going to sue De Lucca."

"It bothered me all the way home, Buddy. My God, I know it isn't your grandfather. I mean, that's preposterous. I love your grandfather, and a lot of people play *Tosca*. Daddy loves *Tosca* because everyone dies in the end."

"De Lucca actually thinks Gentlehands *is* my grandfather!"

"He's going to get himself in a lot of trouble, Buddy. . . . Am I in trouble, with you?"

"Not if you round up a dozen towheads," I said.

"I'll go to work on it, Buddy. Will you come by when you're through?"

I said I would, and when I went back on the floor, I told Kick she wanted maple walnut ice cream for the party. I knew we'd run out that morning.

"Postpone it," he said. "Stall her until tomorrow."

The only newspaper we carried in Sweet Mouth was *The Seaville Citizen*, which came out every Tuesday. At noon, the delivery boy dropped fifty copies outside and I went out to retrieve them. I tore off the string, grabbed a copy and read the story, standing on the sidewalk.

102

MONTAUK MAN
ACCUSED OF BEING NAZI

In this Wednesday's *New York Record,* Seaville summer resident, Nicholas L. De Lucca, in a front-page article, will accuse Frank O. Trenker of Montauk, of being a former SS officer at Auschwitz, notorious for his acts of cruelty and murder.

De Lucca, 57, a free-lance investigative reporter and occasional stringer for *The New York Record* city desk, has a personal interest in forcing an investigation into Trenker. His cousin, Roselina De Lucca, died at Auschwitz. De Lucca never met his cousin. She was 15 when she was among the Roman Jews transported from Italy to the infamous Polish concentration camp, in 1943. Information concerning her treatment and death was documented by one of the few Jewish survivors from Rome.

On the basis of information provided by an Austrian Nazi-hunter, De Lucca has been in pursuit of Trenker through many countries, for three years. According to De Lucca, there is no statute prohibiting the admittance of a war criminal, but all immigrants upon entrance to America must sign a statement declaring that they did not participate in the persecution of a minority because of race, creed or national origin. De Lucca's intention is to stimulate official action against Trenker on the basis that Trenker falsely signed this statement, and is subject to denaturalization and ultimate extradition to West Germany.

The New York Record alleges that Trenker was known by the ironic nickname "Gentlehands" at Auschwitz, because of his habit of playing often an aria from the opera *Tosca,* *"O dolci mani,"* to torment the homesick Italian females.

The article describes a day when young Roselina De Lucca sneaked the collar off a dead guard dog, thought to be poisoned by a prisoner. ("The raggedy, ill, cold and hungry inmates had learned that everything was useful: string to tie up their shoes, old rags to wrap around their frozen feet, anything with which to barter for something to help them stay alive, and this child had found a way to secure the collar of the dead dog.") After she was forced to stand naked in the snow, as an example, for two hours, Trenker then offered her a warm coat and hot soup. On her way to get them, according to the article in *The Record,* Trenker, a member of the SS, sicked the surviving attack dog on her.

Little is known about Trenker in Montauk. A shopkeeper described him as a good-hearted man who loves animals and always has a smile and a friendly word for others. Many spoke of his strikingly handsome appearance, and the article mentions the fact Trenker was one of the youngest SS officers at Auschwitz, known for his imposing good looks.

Most citizens interviewed asked not to be named, but the overall feeling exists either that it could not possibly be Trenker ("Not that man—he wouldn't hurt a fly!"), or that if indeed Trenker was an officer in the SS, and all that the article claims, "It was a long time ago. The past is over. Let the poor man be. He's not hurting anyone."

I was still standing on the sidewalk, finishing the article, when my father pulled up in the Toyota.

"Get in!" he said. He reached across and opened the door for me.

Streaker was in the backseat.

"I've got three more hours, Dad."

"Get in, Buddy!" He pounded the empty seat beside him with his fist.

I still had on my apron, and my sweater was hanging up in the employees' room, but I got in, and my father took off. I'd left the copies of *The Citizen* outside Sweet Mouth, except for the one I had in my hand.

"Did you read it?" my father said.

"It's a mistake, Dad." I started to explain that I couldn't just walk out on Kick, either, during the lunch hour, and my father cracked his fist down on the steering wheel this time, and told me to keep my mouth shut.

"We haven't been mentioned," my father said, *"yet.* But your mother's a wreck!"

"It isn't Grandfather," I said; I almost laughed at the idea, but my father punched the steering wheel again and barked, "The hell it isn't!"

"That damn Nazi," Streaker said.

"Shut up, Streaker!" my father said.

104

I had to look out the window to get control of myself. I had to try to talk to myself the way Grandpa would talk something through with me, staying cool, figuring it out rationally: it was a fact people were often unfair and mean, and my father was certainly a person who leaned far over in that direction, so what did I expect him to react like after he read that article? And now I just had to concentrate on keeping *my* head.

"What do you think of your grandfather now?" my father said, as though he'd never heard me say it was a mistake, it wasn't him. "Are you proud of him?"

I knew he wasn't really looking for answers to his questions.

"Did you take his jeep this morning, Buddy?"

I nodded.

"Answer me, Buddy!"

"You're not interested in my answers," I said. "You listen because you want to hear that you're right, so you can't hear that you're wrong."

"Did - you - take - his - jeep - this - morning?" my father said, very slowly, his eyes bugging out with rage.

"I take it every morning."

"You used to take it every morning!" said my father.

"You stop taking it," Streaker said.

"Leave it where you left it," my father said.

"Leave it where you left it, Buddy," Streaker joined in.

"I won't need any transportation after today, anyway," I said. "I'll be fired for this little number, leaving Kick during the lunch rush."

"That story just breaks my heart," my father said. "After what I just read in *The Citizen*, your story just breaks my heart."

I said it very softly. "It's not Grandfather, Dad. Don't you think I know Grandfather by now?"

"No I don't think you know Grandfather by now, or anything else! You were interested in producing a fancy relative to impress Miss Gottbucks from Beaublahblah, well, you produced one for her, didn't you?"

"We can't talk," I said.

"You're damn right we can't!"

"Is Buddy going to live with us again?" Streaker asked.

"Buddy is going to stay home from now on," my father said, "whether Buddy likes it or not!"

16

The only thing my mother seemed to care about was whether or not our name would be brought into the "scandal." She wasn't interested in anything I had to say about Grandpa Trenker's innocence.

"He was *there,* in Germany," she said. "None of them were innocent."

"He didn't have anything to do with those concentration camps," I said.

"Oh Buddy, he was a German!"

"Loyal to his own," I said, "just the way you claimed you were loyal to your own, the other night in Montauk, when we were talking about the Vietnam war!"

"Loyal to his own?" She gave a snide hoot. "His own were over here in America scratching for a living!"

"You know what I mean," I said. "He was loyal to his country."

"Some country!"

"You once said you'd have disowned me if *I'd* refused to go to Vietnam!"

"Buddy, this is not the same thing," she said.

"Why isn't it?"

"I'm sorry I ever went to Montauk and sat down at his table!" she said, ignoring my question. "I did that for *you,* Buddy. Now you do something for me. Stay away from him! I don't want to hear his name in this house!"

"We're great Americans!" I said. "He's guilty before he's had a chance to prove he's innocent!"

"You heard your mother," my father said. He was strapping on his gun, getting ready to leave for work. Big deal, I thought as I watched him; a lot he knows or cares about the law!

Streaker was curled up on the couch biting his nails, pretending he was watching a rerun of *Sesame Street*.

This time I didn't even try to reason with my mother, or try to make it all right with Streaker that I was leaving. I waited until my father drove off, and my mother carried a load of wash down to the basement. Then I took off for Fireplace Road, hitching a ride to the parking lot behind the A&P where I'd left the jeep.

It was about two thirty when I got to Beauregard. It was one of those fantastic summer days, and I didn't wait for Peacock to let me in. I knew everyone would be sitting around the pool. I walked down the side of the house, and called Skye's name. I had no intention of staying there that afternoon. I wanted to be with my grandfather, and I wanted Skye to go to Montauk with me.

Og Pennington saw me coming, got up from a chaise, and walked toward me. He was in swimming trunks, rubbing some Bonnie Bell Sure Tan Gel into his chest. "Skye isn't here, but I'd like to talk with you, Buddy."

"Where is she?"

"She rounded up some kids at the beach to take to Sweet Mouth for sundaes. Did you get off early?"

"Sort of," I said, and he put an arm around my shoulder, an unusual gesture for him, and steered me down the walk to the pool. "You'd only miss Skye if you tried to connect with her now. I'd like to say something."

Lennie Waterhouse was down at the other end of the pool. He looked up from a copy of some paperback he was reading, gave a wave, then flopped over on his stomach and fixed the book under his nose.

"We can talk privately," Og said, pointing to a director's chair. "Sit down, Buddy, would you?"

"I can't stay."

"I don't blame you for being upset. I read *The Citizen*."

I sat down.

"It isn't my grandfather," I said. "It's a mistake."

"I can see why you'd want to think that, Buddy." He

108

stretched his long legs out in front of him, and ran his fingers through his coal-colored hair.

"I think that, because it isn't my grandfather," I said.

"Buddy, you might not like De Lucca, I don't *like* him, either, but I respect him because he's sharp, too sharp to get *The Record* or *The Citizen* into a libel suit."

"Well that's what he's done."

Og reached out and picked up a folder from the wrought-iron table in front of him. "I just read a copy of his article in *The Record*."

"I don't care what you just read."

He slapped the folder across his bare knees. "A man can't print this kind of material without being absolutely sure, Buddy! Don't you think *The Record* checked the story out?"

"There've been mistakes like this before," I said.

"I wish you'd read just a few things. I've marked a few things."

"Why should I read lies?"

"Read this," he said, "unless you're afraid to read it. Here, where I've marked it in red."

I took the folder from him. Halfway down the first page, he'd drawn a line beside this paragraph:

Ninety-nine persons had been squeezed into the cattle car, including many youngsters younger than Roselina De Lucca. . . . A scorching sun beat down on the roof, and the inside of the car became suffocating. . . . The passengers were mostly families of good standing in the community, people of culture, but as the hours passed the pressure built. Those who had to relieve themselves had no facilities, no choice but to urinate and defecate where they stood. The stench was unbelievable. Babies cried and old people moaned, and the sick begged for water, air; and fear increased until there was a bedlam inside the car, speeding out of Rome, out of Italy, their destination unknown to them.

"This hasn't got anything to do with my grandfather," I said.

"All right then, read it," Og said. "It won't take long. I've marked some passages."

I glanced at another on the second page.

Immediately after they left the cattle cars at Auschwitz, they were marched past Renner and Trenker who sorted them with a glance. Condemned to death were: all mothers together with children up to age thirteen, the pregnant, the deformed, invalids, the sick (even the exhausted who only seemed sick after the torturous ride there), and all men and women over fifty.

I let out my breath and said again, "It wasn't him." Og pointed to a passage at the bottom of the page.

A group of naked women, some pregnant, some carrying babies, were about to enter the gas chamber. Somehow Trenker learned that one of the young girls had been a singer. He ordered her to sing for him, and dance to her song. As she did, she seized Renner's gun and shot him in the leg. Renner survived. Trenker sicked his dog on the girl. It was his favorite death sentence.

I handed the folder back to Og. "I'm not going to read any more." I thought I might get sick, and I felt like just puking in their pool.

"Buddy," Og said, "if there's a chance, as you claim, that this Trenker isn't your grandfather—"

I didn't let him finish. "It isn't!" I said.

"Let me finish—even if it isn't, this is very strong stuff. There's more, much more. How do you think people are going to react when this comes out on Sunday?"

"What do you want from me?" I said. "I'm telling you my grandfather had nothing to do with that!"

"What I want from you is some consideration for my sister."

"How about some consideration for my grandfather?" I said.

"We're willing to give him the benefit of the doubt, innocent until proven guilty," Og said, "but why drag

110

Skye into this? Skye could get hurt, do you realize that?"

"Your family doesn't want me to see her, is that it?"

"We don't want her going there," Og said. "Don't take her there, even if she wants to go."

"I wouldn't let anything happen to her," I said.

"You wouldn't be able to prevent it," he said. "Don't take her there."

"All right," I agreed.

"We like you, Buddy," he said.

"Oh thanks," I said.

"Don't be sarcastic. You don't have to be sarcastic."

"He never did anything to Skye," I said, "but try to please her; make her dinner, play tapes for her."

"She told us all that. That isn't the point."

"The point is now he's in trouble because some friend of your family's made a mistake, so the hell with him!"

"De Lucca's not a friend of our family's," Og said. "Mother hardly knows him."

"But you all believe him."

"We believe Skye could be in danger going there," he said.

Then Peacock appeared to see if I wanted something cool to drink, which I didn't, and I stood up. I could see Mrs. Pennington, in a blue-and-white sundress, stepping out from the pool house, glancing up in our direction, then moving back in, out of sight.

"Tell your family not to worry," I said.

"Let's shake on it," he said, and he pumped my limp hand up and down, let go, and I left.

When I arrived in Montauk, my grandfather was working in the rock garden, down by the steps to the ocean. There was a copy of *The Citizen* on the table beside his chair.

I watched him for a while, from the window. I wanted to go out and say something to him . . . that I was there for once because he needed me, not because I needed him . . . and that all the way out there I'd been remembering a poem I'd memorized once for

English. At the time I'd thought it was a little hysterical, or heavy—it certainly wasn't something I automatically identified with. Suddenly it had meaning, and I knew it by heart, and I wished I could just for once in my life use something I'd learned for school, for real. It was called "If" by Rudyard Kipling.

> *If you can keep your head when all about you*
> *Are losing theirs and blaming it on you;*
> *If you can trust yourself when all men doubt you,*
> *But make allowance for their doubting too;*
> *If you can wait and not be tired by waiting,*
> *Or being lied about, don't deal in lies,*
> *Or, being hated, don't give way to hating,*
> *And yet don't look too good, nor talk too wise . . .*

That was the first verse. The point of the poem was that if you could manage to do all those things, and a lot more described in the other verses, you'd come out a man. A lot of the guys thought it was too macho when I read it. I'd really just picked it out because I knew it was the kind of thing my teacher, Mr. Kersen, would go for. But that afternoon I was glad I still knew it, because it said a lot to me about Grandpa Trenker.

The only thing I could think to do, since I couldn't say the things I wanted to say to him, was carry on the way we always had. I took a shower and changed into clean clothes, and I played with Graham. When the phone rang, I answered it for him. I could see him through the window as he heard the ring and headed up to the house. He probably didn't know I was there.

"Hello?" I said.

"I hope you burn in hell the way you burned the Jews, you filthy Nazi!"

There was a click, then the dial tone. I put the phone down.

"Well, hello, Buddy! Who was that?" he said as he came inside.

"Wrong number," I said. My insides were still twisted with shock.

"Another one of those calls, hmmm?" He took off his gloves and sighed.

112

I nodded.

"Take the telephone off the hook," he said. "Put the pillow over it."

He rubbed his eyes with his fingers a moment. "Does your family know you're here?"

I lied and said they did.

"They don't approve of your being here, do they?"

"They left it up to me," I said, wishing that were true, wishing they were any way but the way they were. As far as I was concerned, right then and there, my grandfather was the only family I cared about anymore, and I cared about him a whole lot. I wanted to try and give back a little of what he'd given me, even if it just meant being with him as much as I could, letting him know that way I was sticking by him.

We sat around for a while talking about letting Graham go. He wanted to do it right away, that night. I knew we should, but I hated putting Graham out at a time when everything seemed to be going against my grandfather. Graham had become like his lapdog, and he followed him around and watched him, and even carried over tapes to my grandfather for him to play, and stroked his cheeks sometimes when he listened to opera on the back of my grandfather's chair.

"We must do it, Buddy," said my grandfather. "There's something else, too." He stood up to let Mignon out, then paced around the room as he talked. "If anything should happen to me, remove the animal feeders. It's still summer, and there's still time for them to look in new places for their food. When it gets colder, there isn't time for that, nor for them to find new territories. Do you understand?"

"Nothing is going to happen to you," I said flatly. It was as close as I could come, I guess, to telling him I loved him.

"I said if, Buddy." He smiled and touched my head gently with his hand. "There's an if in all our lives."

My grandfather broiled some flounder for dinner, which we had with fresh corn from his vegetable garden. He poured me a glass of white wine, and we didn't talk a lot, but listened to music and watched the ocean.

We were just finishing when we heard a car horn honking.

"Skye?" he said.

"I don't think so," I said, but even though I knew the sense to what Og had said, I hoped it *was* her.

There was a more persistent honking then, and both my grandfather and I went to the back door. It kept on, and we walked out into the yard together. The sun was setting, turning the sky bright pink and deep blue.

"That sounds like the horn on my Alfa," said my grandfather.

As we went down toward the driveway, we heard tires squeal, and a car took off.

I think we both thought someone had stolen his car. But as we walked closer we saw both the jeep and the Alfa Romeo. The door of the Alfa Romeo was open, and its sides were soaped with swastikas.

In the front seat, her fur soaked with blood, was Mignon. Her throat was slit. Her dead eyes stared back at us. Above her, attached to the steering wheel, a crude sign hung: NAZI DOG!

17

After we found Mignon dead, my grandfather insisted that I pack my things and go home immediately. He was afraid for my safety.

"What about you?" I said.

"I'll take care of myself, but I can't do that as well worrying about you, Buddy."

"Isn't there something I can do?"

"One thing," he said. He wrote something on a piece of paper. "I've been late getting off something to someone. I'll give you this number in New York to call. Make the call in the morning." He reached into his pocket, then put a five-dollar bill in my hand. "Tell whoever answers the phone that the package from Trenker is on the way. I don't want to use my own phone. It may be tapped. There's no sense involving innocent people in all this."

I pocketed the money for the call, and the slip of paper with the number on it. "Can I call *you* tomorrow, too, to see if you're okay?"

"I don't think that's wise, Buddy, for the same reason."

"Can I come here after work?"

He shook his head from side to side. "I'll be all right, though. This thing will run its course. We'll wait until it does, and meanwhile, enjoy the jeep."

I tried to get him to let me stay long enough to help him bury Mignon, and set Graham free, but he was firm. He put his long arm around my shoulder and walked me down the driveway. Before I drove off, I wanted to put my arms around him, although I didn't even do that anymore with my father. We stood there for a moment, then he stuck out his hand and we shook.

"I'll see you soon," I said. "Nothing better happen to you!"

There were tears starting to roll down my cheeks, and he stopped one with his finger. Then he put his hand down.

I saw him, through the rearview mirror, watching me as I pulled away.

When I got home, my father was still on duty. My mother made me take the jeep up to the next street, park it there, and walk back, so my father wouldn't know I'd run off.

Streaker was in bed. I sat down in the living room and told my mother what had happened to Mignon. I thought I was going to bawl again. I hadn't cried so much in front of my mother since I was Streaker's age.

My mother waited for me to finish and just looked at me for a minute.

"Do you expect me to feel sorry for his dog after what he let dogs do to human beings?" she said. "Oh, *Buddy*."

"Can't you get it through your head it isn't him?"

"Frank O. Trenker is him!" she said. "Tomorrow, you take that jeep back to the A&P parking lot where it was this morning, and stay out of his life!"

"He said I could use it."

"I don't care what he said. We don't want anything from a Nazi!"

"Now I can't talk to you, either," I said.

"Why do you always give *him* the benefit of the doubt?" she said. "Why is it your father and I are always wrong and your grandfather can do no wrong in your eyes?"

"Because I *know* him!" I said.

"Oh and you don't know us?"

"I'm beginning to think I don't."

"Go to bed, Buddy," she said. "If your father comes home and hears that kind of talk, he'll knock your block off."

116

I stood up.

"Don't discuss this with Streaker," she said. "I'm worried about him. He's heard Nazi this and Nazi that, and you've been running off whenever you've felt like it. That kid's going to be a mess if this doesn't stop!"

"That's right," I said. "Let's all worry about Streaker for a change."

"We worry about you, too," she said. "Your father fixed everything with Kick. You'll still have your job tomorrow."

"That's just what I feel like doing tomorrow," I said.

"And Buddy, don't mention any of this to Kick or Ollie or anyone! We don't want our name involved, do you understand?"

"Perfectly," I said.

"It's bad enough that the Penningtons know our connection by now," she said. "Well, I've never met your girlfriend, anyway. I'm not good enough to meet her, I guess. We don't travel in the same circles."

"You could say that," I said.

"I could care less about *their* circle," she said. "That's *your* hang-up, Buddy Boyle!"

I almost knocked Streaker over when I opened the door to our bedroom. He'd been crouched there listening to everything.

"Who killed the dog, Buddy?"

"People," I said, getting out of my clothes. "Get up in your bunk, Streaker."

"How did they kill her?"

"They killed her. Isn't that enough for you? Do you want all the gory details?"

"Were they Nazis, too?"

"What's a Nazi, Streaker?"

"A killer!"

"How do *you* know what a Nazi is?"

"Because your grandfather is a Nazi and he killed people. He's a German!"

I put out the light and got in the bunk under Streaker.

"Listen, Streaker," I said. "He's our grandfather, not my grandfather, *ours*. We're *half* German."

117

"He's not my grandfather."

"And he's one of the kindest people I've ever known!"

"But he's not my grandfather and I'm not half German."

"You're half German, all right. Mrs. Schneider up on Underwood is German. You better not eat those fudge brownies of hers anymore, they might be poisoned."

"She's not German."

"Yes she is, Streaker," I said, "and your grandfather is a very good man people are telling lousy lies about!"

"He's not mine and he's not good," Streaker said. "That's *your* hang-up, Buddy Boyle!"

Kick wasn't there when I got to Sweet Mouth the next day. We were getting another rainy day, so business was off: people were sleeping late. I waited until nine thirty, then got some change and went down to the telephone booth in the A&P parking lot. I fed the toll and waited for the ring, and a woman answered.

"Stanton Stamp Shop."

"Is this 212 324-4513?"

"Yes."

"The package from Trenker is on the way."

"Thank you," she said.

Even though he'd told me not to, I stuck another coin in and dialed my grandfather's number. I got a busy signal. I figured he probably had the phone off the hook again. . . . It was too early to call Skye.

Kick came in about quarter to ten, smiling and relaxed, high again. He began talking with a couple who were trying to eat their eggs in peace.

He was doing a monologue. ". . . so these Nazis surrounded this old Berlin Jew and said, 'Tell us, Yid, who caused the war?' Well, the old Jew was no fool, so he said, 'The Jews,' and then he added, 'and the bicycle riders.' The Nazis were puzzled. 'Why the bicycle riders?' The old Jew shrugged his shoulders. 'Why the Jews?' "

Kick laughed for a long time at his own joke, and

then he said to the man, "We've got an SS guy right out here in Montauk. How do you like that?"

"I read about it," the man mumbled. The woman's expression was getting more and more steamed.

"They always have gardens," Kick said. "Did you ever notice? They have gardens and an American flag waving in their front yards and people say, 'Why Mr. Puffundstart couldn't be a Nazi! He grows these lovely red roses and his petunia beds don't have a weed in them!' "

The woman looked up then and said sharply, "We're on vacation. We don't care to hear unpleasant things on vacation."

"Please excuse me," Kick said. "And excuse me for the rain, too."

He walked back to where I was standing and whispered in a falsetto, "We're on vacation. We don't care to hear unpleasant things on vacation." He gave my ribs a nudge with his elbow.

I looked at my watch. It was ten o'clock.

"That was a great joke," I said. "They're jackasses, aren't they? Can I please use the phone in your office?"

"That was a great joke, they're jackasses, can I please use the phone in your office? You *are* a *gozlin,* Buddy. . . . Use anything you want. This is my last day here!"

"I'm sorry to hear that," I said.

"No you're not, and no, I'm not," he said.

It took Skye about five minutes to get to the phone.

"Where *were* you last night? Your grandfather's number was busy and I couldn't find your father listed in the local directory." We have an unlisted phone—a lot of policemen in Seaville don't list their phones because of crank calls—but I didn't have to explain because Skye went right on, as always. "I was worried, Buddy. Og told me he talked to you, and I want to tell you right now that I'm going anywhere I feel like going, including out to Montauk with you."

"My grandfather doesn't want us out there. He doesn't think it's safe for us right now."

"Daddy just brought home a copy of *The Record*, Buddy, and I could die!"

"I haven't seen it."

"Your family isn't mentioned, Buddy. De Lucca told my mother he purposely kept your family's name out of what he wrote because he was aware of the estrangement."

"De Lucca's all heart," I said.

"Oh, Buddy, there are photographs and everything. It *has* to be a terrible mistake!"

"It is, and my grandfather's going through hell because of it."

"Would you tell him for me I don't believe it, not a word of it?"

"Okay," I said. "Pick me up after work?"

She said she would, and then Kick appeared in the office. He had an envelope in his hand.

"A small boy just delivered a billet-doux," he said. "Mr. William Boyle, Jr. That's *you*, isn't it, *Gozlin?*"

I took the envelope from his hand.

"I remember when I used to be young and eager, too," Kick said. He sat down and began to roll a joint. "Do you know when I decided I preferred pot to marriage, Buddy-O?"

I hoped it wasn't going to be one of his rambling pot stories. I started to tear the envelope open.

"I decided I preferred pot to marriage when my sweet wife said this SS fellow living out in Montauk was only doing his duty. That's what Mrs. Townsend said. Oh they never call her Mrs. Richards and I'm damn glad, because I told Mrs. Townsend that her mind stinks! Wouldn't you say that her mind stinks like a manure heap, Buddy?"

"Okay," I said.

"What does 'okay' mean?"

"I think somebody ought to be sure he's named the right person," I said.

"Ah!" Kick said. "You're from the 'it-couldn't-be-him-he-grows-such-lovely-roses' school of thought."

"I'd like to read my letter, Kick."

"Go ahead," Kick said, lighting a match. "I'm going

120

to escape these harsh realities. Grass will put you on your ass and make time pass."

I went into the Men's and opened the envelope.

The message from my grandfather was short, and very clear.

I am going away. Take what you want from Montauk. I hope some of what you take will be a good memory of our brief friendship, which gave me great happiness. I know the person you will soon be learning about, only by hearsay now. He is as much a stranger to me as he will be to you. I live in the present between two unfathomable clouds, what was and what will be.

18

Kick was not the only one in Sweet Mouth talking about my grandfather that day. After *The New York Record* appeared in Seaville, customers arrived for late breakfast and early lunch carrying copies of the newspaper. De Lucca's story appeared on the front page, and continued to the second section. Everyone I waited on was discussing it. I didn't have a chance to read it until the crowd thinned out, around two thirty. Then I picked up a copy someone had left on a table.

In the second section there were four photographs. One was a picture of my grandfather, taken thirty years ago in Argentina. It was easy to recognize the younger version of him, carrying a dog, a pipe in his mouth; his hair was darker.

Two of the photographs were linked together in one frame. At the top was a photograph of a burned house; under it, a picture of a woman.

The caption read: *The house of Carlita Fornez (below) located outside Havana, Cuba, was destroyed by a firebomb in 1951, purportedly planted by The Jewish Action League. Miss Fornez was killed, but Trenker, the intended victim, survived.*

The fourth photograph was of a young man in uniform. The caption read: *SS Colonel Dr. Werner Renner, chief physician at Auschwitz. Reported to be somewhere in South America. Renner carefully avoided being photographed after he escaped from Germany in 1945.*

There was more about Renner in the article.

Dr. Werner Renner had two passions, stamp-collecting and carving pipes of wood and meerschaum. While some camp physicians had to drink great quan-

tities of alcohol to tolerate their task of selecting those who were to die in the gas chambers, Dr. Renner, on the other hand, a teetotaler, whittled away on one of his pipes and casually pointed to the doomed men, women and children as they passed in review. . . . It has been rumored that Renner produced meerschaum pipes after the war, which were imported from Turkey, and valued at $5000 and more per pipe.

I remembered the night my grandfather showed Skye his meerschaum pipe. I remembered my grandfather remarking that Mr. Verner was just an old man who still collected stamps like a boy. My grandfather always pronounced his w's like v's. It was not a *Mr.* Verner who called him from time to time. It was Werner Renner.

The article concluded: *Frank Trenker was born into a very strict Roman Catholic family. His father was a bigoted and fanatic man who took a religious oath at the time of his son's birth, dedicating Frank Trenker to God and the priesthood. He directed his entire youthful education toward the goal of making him a priest, forcing him to do penance over the slightest misdeed. When Frank Trenker broke with the church, he joined the NSDAP. He exchanged Catholic dogma for Nazi ideology, and from 1940 on, his only activities as a member of the SS Death Head units were concerned with concentration camps. . . . In early 1944, as Allied armies began their drive for Paris, Trenker and Renner began melting down the gold from jewelry and teeth of Auschwitz victims to ship to Swiss banks. At the end of the war both men escaped through Austria into Italy, and ultimately boarded ships bound for Argentina.*

When Skye picked me up in front of Sweet Mouth she said, "I have to tell you something, Buddy. There's an I.N.S. man looking for your grandfather. De Lucca told my father about it."

"He's left Montauk," I said.

"Oh, *no!* Where is he?"

"I don't know where he is." I had an idea I *did*

123

know, that the "package" on its way to the Stanton Stamp Shop was my grandfather.

Skye and I began riding around in the Jensen, in the rain, while she talked nonstop about him. "I've never heard of anything so gross in my entire life!" she said. "Even Daddy says he has to admire you for sticking by your own in the worst possible circumstances, and anyway, no one's given your grandfather a chance to deny anything! Daddy says if De Lucca *is* wrong, your grandfather will have one hell of a settlement, and Mummy wants you to know she really doesn't know anything about De Lucca. She thought all along he might even be investigating *us*, for taxes or some stupid thing. You can investigate *anyone* and come up with *something!*"

I kept watching her in profile, trying to memorize the way she looked, and telling myself maybe I wouldn't have to, maybe the whole thing would just blow over.

"Og read a case once where a man spent thirty years in prison for a crime he didn't commit, Buddy! He looked almost exactly like the real criminal!"

I was thinking if it hadn't been for trying to impress her, I never would have known him.

If it hadn't been for Skye, I probably would have been doing a number like my mother, snarling around about what a Nazi he was and praying to God the good name of Boyle wouldn't ever be linked with his.

"Did you tell him I don't believe that article, Buddy?" Skye asked me.

"I didn't have the chance."

"I wish he *knew* there were people who believe in him."

"He'll get by."

"What about Mignon and Graham?"

"He set Graham free."

"He took Mignon with him," she said flatly. It wasn't a question I had to answer.

"This could ruin his life," she said.

I didn't say anything.

"I wish there was something we could do," she said.

"There isn't."

"I know it's much worse for you, Buddy."

I didn't answer.

"If someone I loved was falsely accused of a crime, I'd just die!"

"Yeah."

"I would, I'd die, because you feel so helpless and there's nothing you can really do. You have to wait for time to pass and lawyers to do things and all the while you're hurting so."

I shouted what I said next. "Cut it out!"

She gave me one quick, wide-eyed stare of alarm and then got ahold of herself again.

"I thought you'd want to talk about it," she said quietly.

"How long can we talk about it?"

She didn't answer and I didn't add anything. We just continued to drive around aimlessly.

Then she tried to change the subject. I knew she was making this big effort to be understanding.

"Connie Spreckles has a new Connie. He came by this morning in it."

"What's a new Connie?"

"A new Lincoln Continental."

"Oh."

"Everybody calls them Connies."

"Oh," I said. "I didn't know that."

"Don't be sarcastic, Buddy."

"I just wish you could hear yourself sometimes," I said.

She clammed up and we kept driving around.

"I don't know anyone who calls a Lincoln Continental a Connie, that's all."

"A lot of people do."

"Well I'm wrong. I've been wrong before."

"There's nothing awful about calling it a Connie, either," she said.

We kept on going.

"There's a fair at the church," she said.

"There's a fair at the church every year."

"Maybe it would take our minds off this."

"It's a kids' fair."

"I know it's a kids' fair," she said. "I live out here, too, Buddy."

"In the summer you live out here," I said.

"I've been coming out here every summer for fourteen years," she said.

"That's not living out here," I said.

"It's not *not* living out here, either."

"Okay," I said, "you live out here."

I had an idea then. Maybe I got it because I had the feeling things between us were coming to an end, anyway, and why not speed it to its doomed finish? I'd like to say I'd suddenly made the decision to stop wallowing in my misery and start thinking of someone else, like Streaker, but in my right mind I'd never have suggested that Skye come home with me, unannounced, to pick up my brother and take him to St. Luke's Summer Fair. I didn't even know if Streaker was there, or if my father would be sleeping.

"I never even knew you *had* a kid brother!" Skye said. "It sounds like a neat idea!"

It wasn't a neat idea at all. My mother never liked anyone to see the house until she'd pushed the Hoover around for hours beforehand and taken Endust to all the furniture.

I gave her the directions and we headed up Fireplace Road.

On the way there, I turned on the radio so we didn't have to talk. There were two speakers in the back of the Jensen, and I turned up the sound so we were flooded with this steady barrage of top tens the local radio station played.

I remembered the day my Uncle Ted died, my father told my mother he kept hearing Uncle Ted's voice in his mind, hearing his laugh, hearing him sing, hearing him tell Irish jokes. That afternoon in the rain, I kept hearing my grandfather. There was no way I could put him out of my mind.

I'd hear him tell me the names of the wildflowers he'd picked were adder's-tongues, moth mulleins and saxifrages, and then he'd be telling me never to be a weak person. I'd see him leaning back in his chair, saying his life might have been different if he'd met Carla earlier, then explaining to Skye that birds weren't really free, that they were prisoners of their own territory. Everything came rushing back: the night he tried to teach me how to pour wine, and the night he freed Graham from the steel trap. The meals he cooked for me, and the advice he gave me about clothes. I could see him making coffee mornings in his black silk robe, and outside by the steps to the ocean, gardening in his old corduroy pants. Then almost as though he was beside me in the Jensen, I could hear him telling me that once I knew something was wrong, I was responsible—"whether you see it or hear about it, and most particularly when you're a part of it."

I kept remembering the article, too, trying to tie together the old man who was outraged that animals would suffer because women wanted to wear fur coats . . . and the young man who played the aria from *Tosca* to torment the Jewish women and girls homesick for Italy, sicking his attack dogs on them for punishment. . . . Gentlehands, and I could picture his large hands with their long fingers, and watch him reach out and stop a tear rolling down my cheek, the last time we saw each other.

"Here's your street, Buddy," Skye shouted above the music. "What number is your house?"

"It's the little yellow one at the end."

She turned down the music. "I don't want to pull in with that awful music blaring away. Will your mother be there? I think I'm a little nervous, Buddy."

Not as nervous as my mother will be, I thought.

"Is this a good idea, to just surprise her? Mummy hates surprises. She wants everything immaculate and perfect when she meets new people."

"Our mommies are different," I said, but I knew it was probably the only way they were alike.

There was some part of me that even looked forward to the idea of this big disaster number, with my mother trying to control her temper and kick Streaker's toys under things, and pick up my father's old copies of *Gun and Badge* from the floor, and dirty coffee cups from the living-room table, forcing herself to smile at Skye all the while . . . and maybe my father just getting up from a nap in his undershirt, speechless, lighting up a cigar to give himself something to do with his mouth and his hands.

The Toyota was gone. That meant my father was, too.

"Wait a *minute,* Buddy!" Skye said, as I pushed down on the door handle. "Let me comb my hair."

"You look fine," I said. "Nobody else will be all in blue."

"Why do you say something mean like that? I always dress in one color, it's my trademark," Skye said. "What are you trying to do, Buddy?"

I suddenly didn't know. I sat there with the door of the Jensen halfway open, the rain coming in on my trouser leg, trying to think what I was trying to do, or keep myself from doing.

"My grandfather is Gentlehands," I said. "I think I know where he is, and where Werner Renner is, too."

Skye just looked at me. She was holding her comb. There was a long strand of her soft black hair caught in it. I found one once on my jacket, at my grandfather's, after she'd left. I'd wrapped it in a piece of Kleenex and tucked it in my pocket, to keep.

"What did you just say, Buddy?"

"I think I know where they are."

Then I saw my mother running from our house toward us. Her hair was done up in rollers. She had my father's old yellow slicker on over a pair of jeans, and she had on bedroom slippers.

"Oh, Buddy! Thank God!" Her face was all scrunched up as though she was going to cry.

I started to say, "This is Skye, Mom," and she cut me off with a wave of her hand. "There isn't time. I have to get up to Underwood Drive *now,* Buddy!"

"Get in, Mrs. Boyle," Skye said. "I'll take you there."

My mother was already in the backseat.

"It's Streaker," she said. "He ran away as soon as

your father left for work. He's up on Underwood Drive."

"Calm down, Mom," I said. "It's only a block from here."

"Calm down?" she said. "He's throwing rocks through all of Mrs. Schneider's windows, Buddy! He's wrecking her place!"

My mother's mascara was running while she sobbed.

"Why would he want to hurt old Mrs. Schneider?" she asked.

19

Every August at Beauregard, they throw a Future Party. Guests are supposed to come dressed as they see themselves years and years away.

All the uniformed waiters wore long white beards, and the maids had on white wigs. Even Peacock pinned angel's wings on himself.

Mr. and Mrs. Pennington appeared in matching gold suits as citizens of the moon, and the three butterfly dogs were dressed in sequined coats as moonbeams. Og, from neighboring Mars, was in a silver suit.

For a while I watched Connie Spreckles play badminton with Skye. Connie was in a white doctor's coat, with a stethoscope around his neck. Skye had stuffed her white pantsuit to look pregnant. Rachel was there as the first female president, in a red-white-and-blue Aunt Sam suit. Her brother had come as the first male nun.

I was standing on the sidelines, sipping a fresh lemonade. I'd cut out a question mark from heavy cardboard, which I wore like a sandwich board. Even before he sidled up to me, I could smell De Lucca's sickly sweet cologne. He was puffing on the fake cigarette, wearing a blond wig.

"How do you like my transplant, Buddy?"

"I never thought of you as a blond."

"Blonds have more fun."

"I never thought of you that way, either."

Then he said, "They got Renner. You probably know that."

"I read that he's coming to trial."

"He was the big fish, anyway," De Lucca said.

We stood there for a moment watching a waterball

game going on in the pool. De Lucca didn't say anything about the fact the Immigration Service still hadn't found my grandfather. I think he knew I didn't want to talk about it. He gave my arm a squeeze before he moved on.

"Your tip about that stamp shop in New York helped pull him in, Buddy. Thanks."

Then Skye came running up to me, and we hugged as well as we could with those pillows she had tied around her waist between us.

"I hope it's mine," I said.

"No child of mine is going to have a question mark for a father," she laughed. She took a sip of my lemonade, then slipped out of her sandals.

"Race me, Buddy," she said, and she ran up toward the dunes while I half ran, half walked behind her. She waited for me, and we went over them together, and walked down to the edge of the surf, hand in hand. It was one of those very bright, very hot August afternoons, with almost no breeze from the sea. There were sunbathers everywhere, and a lot of people swimming in the ocean. We walked along silently for a while.

"I'm glad you came," she finally said.

"I've been busy."

"Oh I know."

"I have been. We've got a new owner at Sweet Mouth."

"Do you like him?" She didn't wait for my answer. "I wish you'd brought your suit. We could swim."

"I can't stay."

"Not long enough for some supper?" she said. "Cook's made Madrilene Ring with Shad Roe she makes only once a year and it's to die! She does it only for this party."

"Once a year the firemen play the policemen," I said, "and it's tonight. We have a big picnic after."

"Does your father play?"

"He pitches."

"How's Streaker?"

"Busy," I said. "My mother invents all these things

131

for him to do to earn money to pay for Mrs. Schneider's windows."

"She didn't like me, did she?"

"She worried that you didn't like her because she looked so tacky that day."

"I thought you'd call me."

"I thought I would, too."

Skye stopped walking then and dropped my hand. She moved closer to me and touched my face with her fingers. She tried to get me to look back at her while she watched my eyes. When I couldn't, she kissed my mouth, and I could almost feel the old trembling and pull. I heard her sigh softly.

Then suddenly she pushed me backwards, and I stumbled into the water in my shoes, while she laughed and ran down the hard sand by the surf. I threw off my cardboard question mark and went after her, catching her finally up near the dunes. We wrestled around in the hot sand until we were both perspiring and out of breath. Then we just lay back on the sand, staring up at the few puffs of clouds, laughing and panting at the same time.

We finally walked back to the party. I carried her pillows for her.

"I'll be leaving in a week," she said.

"I know."

"Will you come and say good-bye before I go?"

"Maybe."

"You won't," she said. "I know you won't."

"We'll see."

"And I won't write, either, ever," she said, "but I'll want to sometimes."

I handed her the pillows when we reached the back of the pool house. They were the blue-and-white Beauregard ones with the monogrammed *P*'s.

"I'll leave them here for Peacock. Do you think he'll be surprised to find my baby back here on the lawn?"

"Nothing surprises Peacock," I said.

She didn't walk me to the jeep.

*　　*　　*

I hadn't driven the jeep since the morning I read the letter from my grandfather in Sweet Mouth. It had stayed in the parking lot with the keys under the front seat. I'd finally told my father I wanted to return it to Montauk, even though there was no one there. He said that he and Mom and Streaker would pick me up in the Toyota on the way to the game and picnic at six that night. They'd be waiting for me way down at the end of the driveway, where the chain was strung across it.

I got to the house around five thirty. The Alfa Romeo was there. I figured the day my grandfather took off, he'd probably taken a taxi to the Montauk airport, and chartered one of the small planes to take him wherever he was going.

The house was locked. I let myself in with the key on the ring with the car keys.

Somehow, someone else had gotten in ahead of me. There were things strewn everywhere, as though someone had been on a frantic search for something: drawers were pulled out, their contents emptied onto the oriental rug in the living room. Books had been pulled out of the bookcases, tapes, even cups and dishes and silverware had been taken from the shelves in the kitchen and tossed to the floor. Pictures on the wall had been tipped sideways or taken down. Draperies had been yanked off the windows.

I sat down in my grandfather's chair for a moment and looked around at the mess. My mind must have looked that way inside my head, I thought, with everything I once knew about my grandfather knocked down, tramped across and smashed. . . . I'd been there so often when music was playing that it took me a moment before the soft sound of a woman singing reached my ears and registered. Then I heard a closet door shut behind me in the bedroom.

"Who's here?" I asked. I stood up, listening for an answer.

When there wasn't any, I said, "Is it you?"

It was his car in the driveway, of course. He and I had the only keys. It was he who always put on music.

133

I wondered if he had arrived just ahead of me, found the house that way, and locked the door after him.

I began walking toward the bedroom, and the music played louder, not just because I was getting closer.

"Is it you?" I shouted again.

The door of the bedroom was half open. I stood there, looking in. I could see more debris on the rug: clothes flung about, a chair knocked over, bureau drawers hanging open, and the music turned up even more.

A punch of fear hit my stomach as I thought of the possibility he'd gone mad and done all of it himself, and then I felt him just inside the bedroom, just behind the door, waiting for me.

I spoke through the crack in the door, wanting to say, "Grandfather, it's me," but that wasn't what I said. I said, "Gentlehands?"

The door moved. The crack disappeared.

I felt trapped, and to end the awful suspense, I kicked the door wide open with my foot.

A radio fell from the bureau to the floor. I saw Graham leap across to the window, and out through a broken pane.

I never did lure Graham down from the tree outside my grandfather's house. He only watched me with suspicious eyes while I called to him, and backed up higher into the branches of the spruce.

He had done too much to the inside of the house for me to undo, and I didn't try to keep him out by blocking the open window. I walked through the rooms of the house one last time, stepping over the broken and fallen things.

I knew that it was almost six, and that soon my father and mother and Streaker would be waiting for me down at the end of the driveway.

I had a final look at the view from those windows, at the deep green ocean waters with the whitecaps flecked through them, and the gulls sweeping down with the late-afternoon sun making their wings look pink and silver. The bird feeders had been removed from the railing, but there were still some nuthatches and sparrows hopping around hopefully, and a lone belted kingfisher high in the branches of a fir, watching them.

When I turned around to go, I saw the navy blue cashmere sweater Skye had given me, in a heap on the rug, with the twisted tapes of *Madame Butterfly, La Traviata, Tosca* and *Louise* wound around it. I thought of picking up the sweater to take with me, but I didn't. I just wanted to leave everything about that summer behind me.

ABOUT THE AUTHOR

M. E. KERR was born in Auburn, N.Y., attended the University of Missouri and now lives in East Hampton, New York. She is the author of six other novels for young people—*Dinky Hocker Shoots Smack!*; *If I Love You, Am I Trapped Forever?*; *The Son of Someone Famous*; *Is That You, Miss Blue?*; *Love Is a Missing Person*; *I'll Love You When You're More Like Me*; and *Gentlehands* which is published by Bantam.

TALES OF COURAGE

☐ **JOHNNY GOT HIS GUN**   23777/$3.95
When World War II began, it felt like a summer's festival—a time for generosity, boating, singing and above all, innocence. But nine million corpses later, those feelings will have changed dramatically. This war may have begun as a quest for democracy, but Dalton Trumbo will erase that fantasy and take you to the reality of war, with his shocking, brutal and uncompromising honesty.

☐ **THE RED BADGE OF COURAGE**   21011/$1.50
Hailed as the greatest novel of the Civil War, this is the story of a young volunteer named Henry Fleming, who, in his first encounter with war panics and runs, yet finds that he must return to learn the difference between the ideal of heroism and the true valor achieved in positive, responsible action. Read THE RED BADGE OF COURAGE and learn why it has been one of the most widely-read American novels since 1895.

☐ **APRIL MORNING**   24161/$2.95
It is April 19th, 1775. The British redcoats are marching through your town and although you've never before shot a rifle with the aim of killing a man, suddenly you will—you're *there* at the battle of Lexington and the birth of freedom! Howard Fasts classic will transport you to that legendary time, giving you a feeling that you are living that historic battle and the inevitable outcome will feel as though it's happening for the very first time.